Etienne Leroux 18 / 44

Translated from Afrikaans by Cassandra Perrey

1972 Houghton Mifflin Company Boston

For I

All the characters in this book are fictitious,
the first person is not the writer,
the Russian is not a Russian, the park
is not the park in Oranjezicht, I have no
consumption-racked aunt, but the philosophy
is not original.

Contents

The soldier of the State signed his name with a flourish.
And a new life began.

LITTLE OF IMPORTANCE happened in the year 1844; in fact, it must have been one of the most unimportant years in the bloody chronology of man's existence on earth. There was, it is true, a war between France and Morocco, but only until the sixth of September. The following important people died: Sir Francis Burnett of natural causes; the Mormon prophet, Joseph Smith, violently. The Prince de Joinville bombed Tangier and quite possibly several historical monuments, not to mention a few unimportant inhabitants, were blown to kingdom come. (Try as I might, I cannot after a hundred years mourn the bomb-death of a baby; the picture of a dead baby in Vietnam in my morning paper is an appalling sight.)

It was the year Brigham Young selected his successor. Sir Henry Hardinge became Viceroy of India. The Bank of England Charter Act was passed. The Codex Sinaiticus was discovered by Herr Konstantin von Tischendorf. I cannot, for the life of me, become enthusiastic.

It was a gray year and this the 44th year of my life was a gray year and everything around me was gray and monotonous and my lot was the lot of everyone who experiences middle age with dismal reluctance. And then your letter arrived, Miss X, 18-year-old l'inconnue, and even 1844 became a year of special significance. Eighteen forty-four becomes instantly a year of tremendous importance. It is not a year in which great personalities were immortalized by momentous errors of judgment; it is not a year in which the bones augured significant world events; it is the still year in which things of supreme importance are happening to two strangers like us. A baby dies in Tangier; behind a pillar in the market a Bedouin kisses his beloved in the shadow. I find your letter in your unformed handwriting on my desk and something stops me from throwing it into the wastepaper basket. I open it and start reading and the radio is playing that Charles Segal tune (do you know it?): "It was a great year and will not come again."

The Cottage by the Sea

DOWNS SLOPE to the sea, smelling of decay, and there are geraniums and adderwort and red, yellow, purple, pink and scarlet begonias at Monterville and a whole row of agapanthus that reminds one of George. George, George — I had an aunt who lived there, a member of one of the better-known families, and they thought she had tuberculosis and then her father, that respected man of the district, said that champagne at eleven o'clock in the morning was the civilized way of whetting one's appetite, because the consumptive should gain weight and she should be in a tranquil frame of mind because what is tuberculosis but a by-product of incorrect breathing as a result of emotional disturbance? My thin, aristocratic aunt, stretched out on the chaise longue, the novel in her hand open to the important page thirty which would determine whether she would read further, her eyes fixed on me as, at her feet, I tasted the last drops of Mumm Cordon Rouge from an egg cup. "Y, Y," she said to me, "you should become a writer, one day, and write novels like this one," and her slim fingers turned the book so that I came face to face with the girl on the cover, an Angélique of thirty-two years ago, and I saw the face of my aunt beside the face of Angélique who was later to take form again as you, Miss X, and my beloved Russian, and who was, in the erotic-dream nights of my puberty, to make me sleep with terror on my thin aunt and with lust in the sheaths of a thousand other Angéliques.

On a cloudy day one can easily see the end of the sea from the compact cottage designed by my friend the homosexual architect; when it is white-hot, the sea is pure boundlessness; anything between brings limitation. I used to write for both my thin aunt and Angélique, and in the confusion I achieved that limitation which made me a cheap best-seller writer and which enabled me to have the cottage built by the homosexual architect; but deep within me I dreamed dreams in which my consumptive aunt and you, Angélique, were interwoven layer upon layer like a smorgasbord.

For 44 years I have been seeking a synthesis, dear Russian and dear nymph, for 44 years, and suddenly I am afraid. The Russian's eyes are yellow; her Slavic blood surges red-hot while her husband, the Cossack, races through the snow with saber drawn. She hates teen-age nymphs, like you, X, who arrogantly make your teen-age demands; you forgive her with the disdain of the young. Do you know that she has a fear that you do not have? She is lovely, my Russian, but she dares not let one single moment slip away unmarked. She is Nuits St. Georges and you are vin ordinaire. Both of you make your demands: she, because every year must have meaning for her; you, because, as a nymph with a craving of fire, you impatiently await the initiation, the ritual to which all nymphs are entitled.

Shall I tell you something about the 44-year-old who looks out over the ocean from his snow-white house? Shall I spoil the butterfly flight of his thoughts with the banality of his words? I shall tell you, rather, about the eleven

4

nuns who appeared on the silver-white sand of the deserted beach one misty evening: slender novices whose slenderness not even the cloth could disguise. They were striking poses, stretching their hands out over the ocean, skipping toward the water, bending down to the water, challenging the water right up to their feet and then skipping back in boots, the esoteric nymphs of God. Eleven motionless penguins and then at the next count there were only ten. Under the eyes of the 44-year-old hack in his harris tweed jacket, with the binoculars held up to his face, and in his heart the mutilated gift of God.

Behind a rock, the eleventh novice had lifted her dress three inches to remove her boot and shake a little stone out of it. The hack's heart was deeply moved, but all he could do was pour a whiskey and soda.

The Russian and I arranged to meet in one of the quietest and least-known parks in the city and I was there half an hour early to await my Russian. And what a heavenly, neglected park, with rubber trees, and oaks, and benches under giant poplars that stretch their muscles against the aching blue of the sky! Could they know, those elegant, idle bourgeois women with their dogs snuffling around the trees . . . could he know, that man on the bench who was watching me and who surely follows me everywhere with his cold eyes behind dark glasses (a spy for the Cossack?) . . . could they know, that couple around the corner among the cannas, that the 44-year-old who walked so sprucely through the dew-fresh grass in his suede shoes also had a rendezvous — but what could be keeping her? There was a deserted green pagoda and a phantom orchestra from a previous decade started playing in the hack's imagination. And he was sitting once more next to his consumption-racked aunt, that enchantress of *courtoisie,* listening to the drums and the trumpets, and he saw again the gray marionette conductor who turned around after the crescendo finale and curled his mustache between his thumb and forefinger and looked lightning-flash blue into her eyes so that she moved her fan faster and faster and pressed her nephew to her with a slender arm and said: "Remember, Y, Y, a gentleman admires women, a rogue understands women." Those clichés of my consumption-racked aunt whom the great god Phthisis pared down to subtler beauty but never to destruction.

He was to see her die, eons later, of an undefined disease, and by then he was a reasonably successful hack, and there was a smile in her eyes when she delivered her final deathbed message with one of his novels open beside her bed: "That's not what I meant, Y, Y." There was never great sadness, just a hint of sadness, before the tremendous wisdom of approaching death. "Yet perhaps, who knows. . ." And with a blotched, aged arm and hand she motioned him to leave, to leave, because her exit should be like champagne. "She died quietly," reported the peasant nurse who was accustomed to the protest of the *canaille.*

My Russian stood before me and her dress was aquamarine and behind her was the deserted pagoda, and above her the sun slashed through the gleaming leaves. She allowed me to admire her: the silhouette against the blinding light, and her yellow eyes flashing yellow-warm against the shivering foliage and her lips tasting like the wine of the holy one, the delicious evil blood of his dragon.

We threw questions at each other with the intense curiosity of newborn middle-aged love. (My Russian is 44, like me, and like my aunt of the champagne, years ago.) It was a civilized search: she was honest and admitted to her Slavic passion and her selfishness; she saw me against the background of her fiery romantic demands; and I admitted to my own weaknesses, which are refinement and fear, and it was at once tragic and comic that she transformed my weakness into the sensitive fearlessness of her own world, because she does not know mine, symbolized by the white cottage designed by my friend the homosexual architect. "I am afraid," I said. "I am also afraid," she repeated, but that was the fear of an unknown continent, of an involved history of terror and blood, against the blood and simplicity of my own.

And then I saw the Cossack over her shoulder. I saw him through the pillars of the deserted pagoda, the mighty horseman without his horse, the two henchmen flanking him forming two points of the triangle, their gorilla bodies lithe beneath silk, the knots of their fists like clubs in and out between light and shadow, light and shadow. She could not see the terror in my eyes: her cheek was warm and soft against mine; her hair caressed my temple; her one arm was draped slenderly over my shoulder. I looked at the scene through the Cossack's eyes; and derived a masochistic pleasure from the impending Götterdämmerung in a sunny park where elegant women take their chows and poodles to frisk and rest; and saw the Cossack without snow on yellow, dry ground on his way to a dénouement behind a deserted pagoda, where the Victorian conductor shone his blue eyes upon my consumptive aunt.

And suddenly the park began to waltz, and I was filled with love, with the soft Russian in my arms.

I might have been a good writer; what has . . . whatever has Jesus Christ done to me?

He also warns me, the God of love, against love.

When I walk back, down along the avenue, after meeting my Russian, I look into people's faces and I suddenly feel guilty, because it seems as if the Russian were still in my arms, and I am certain they can see her, and then I realize that this is impossible, naturally, and I smile. A beggar with a dirty handkerchief around his head, his limbs angular like a spider, saw my smile and stretched out his hand. I gave him more than he expected, in penance, and he turned his back on me after receiving the money — blessed man, without commitments and free within the bonds of his diseased body. I am sated with love after being with my Russian and my immediate intention is not to see her again and I enjoy the detachment of the city as I wander around among people completely alone. The indifference of people does not make me feel alone as it usually does; I take pleasure in the rat race and a creative muse sings within me and sharpens my eyes to those novels I want to write and have not yet written. I walked past a dead man whose corpse awaited the ambulance which would bear him to the morgue and I had to elbow my way through the inquisitive pavement spectators who circled courteously to give new arrivals their turn to have a look. In my favorite bar I look at Mrs. Gorgon's mournful eyes and I am sure she can smell the Russian's perfume on me, because she smiles and grows more despondent while she serves whiskey and soda, because Mrs. Gorgon's romantic days are done and she lives only in the

8

warmth of drunken friendship and drunken blindness for her "romantic days" which are done. Before I reach the white cottage by the sea where my deaf, crippled, manic-depressive wife awaits me, I look at the estate belonging to the Princess Ira von Liebenstein and I imagine that I can see her again among the heather (but it is not so, and no princess lives there and the estate is disintegrating) — Princess Ira with the wind in her hair and the blue of the sea in her eyes, and I have forgotten my Russian and I long suddenly for wheat fields where, as a child, I was bitten on the arm by a button spider. "Y, Y," said my aunt, drunk on champagne, "button spiders in this part of the world are different from those in the Swartland. It takes *far* longer to die, poppet." How fascinated she was, my drunk aunt, by the swelling of her nephew's arm, and it was then she told him that only the female bites. Beautiful, glorious wheat fields that my rich uncle planted as much for aesthetic pleasure as for profit. And then I stop in front of my white cottage where my deaf, crippled, manic-depressive wife hangs reproachfully from her crutches. "Why don't you write?" she asks accusingly, just as at other times she accusingly asks, "Can't you stop writing?"

"No," I told the Russian in my arms in front of the deserted pagoda, "she is not jealous; we understand each other" — knowing, naturally, that it was difficult for her to move from one place to another, because it was a complicated process getting her into a car, and that I was completely safe and that she would continue to support me for years to come however dearly I paid for the accusations, and bitterness, and the banality of a petty bourgeois brain

9

inherited from a Swartland butcher-father with heaps of money raked in from intestines and offal. (How many times did he not prove to me, irrefutably, that meat sales barely covered costs?) "Yes," said my aunt when I told her about the coming wedding. "Yes," she said, "and you will pay a good deal. Yet, in the long run — given a little imagination . . ." And she flickered her eyes (she was then 44 and I old enough to appreciate the play). "Yes, it may be possible."

"No," I told the Russian in my arms while I looked at the green pagoda, so strange and desolate in this desolate park. "No." But I did not tell her how much security has come to mean to me ever since I turned 44 and can now sit quietly in my white cottage by the sea and watch driftwood on the beach through an expensive pair of binoculars. "I love you, Y, Y," she said, and brought her eyes very close to mine so that everything went out of focus and the iris dissolved into tiny lines and the red veinlets on the white into rivulets of blood. "How I love you! And how remote you are at times!" And she drew her face back so that everything came into focus again, her lovely yellow eyes and the green on her eyelids, against the background of the deserted pagoda where the Cossack and his two henchmen had just appeared: three specks behind three pillars.

"It's a feeling of loneliness that comes over me," I told her once, but it was in fact the image of my deaf, crippled, manic-depressive wife.

"The aloneness of a writer," she said, satisfied, my dear Russian, with the Lara theme and *Dr. Zhivago* in mind. And in an extraordinary way the Omar Sharif image suits me, as I have retained the melancholy eyes of a child — as well as something of a child's unscrupulousness. Then I decided to tell her about your letters, Miss X. How gloriously jealous she was! A tigerish Russian with incandescent yellow under green. How glorious was the forgiveness when I told her that I had never seen you, and that I did not want to see you.

"Just the situation for a writer," she said at last, convinced.

"I shall write a book about the three of us," I said.

"Be good to me when you write it," said the Russian, exultant.

We kissed so passionately that a squat little woman with a trained Alsatian turned her back on us furiously and made the dog do three tricks, quick as a flash, in front of the deserted, green pagoda. Three times he leapt over the railings, lay down, barked and growled at his mistress' command and abased himself on her instructions while the Russian and I ran our tongues against each other's. Then an innocent milkman came by (innocent in the sense that he was not on his way to commit a robbery, but merely to deliver milk) and the raging dog attacked him instantly and tore his trousers and gnawed white gashes in his black skin. "Down! Down, Rex, down!" shrieked the woman in terror, and beat her little stick on the yellow earth of the park. "Down!" She shieked her rage against me and Russian, who were melting into each other's arms and nibbling at each other's ear lobes. "Down!" she shrieked desperately, and vanquished the animal who ripped a final tear in the trousers and then reluctantly lay down and snarled while the milkman stumbled away dragging his leg. "Bad boy, Rex," caroled the little woman while she glared at us maliciously and rapped her stick on the ground. And the Russian pulled her lips away from mine and whispered in my ear: "She didn't even apologize to the boy."

My Russian has a social conscience.

Then she said: "Tell me about your teen-ager and her teen-age letters."

And then, Miss X, I told her the whole story because you are no more than an X to her and it is unlikely that she will ever meet you in this life.

The First Letters from X

YOUR FIRST LETTER (I could tell by the handwriting that you were an art student), written on both sides of foolscap sheets, carelessly torn out, creased as if you had first read the letter over and over to yourself, began: "Mr. Y, Mr. Y, Mr. Y . . ."

(How I later came to appreciate the incantation of that refrain!)

"Mr. Y, may I write to you and will you write back to me? I am 18 years old, I am an art student, I am still reasonably a virgin and bored, and then I thought — it should be interesting to write to a writer, he ought to write back interesting letters . . ."

I was looking out over the sea where as late as nine o'clock on these summer evenings the sun sets in languid indolence and a final intense radiance. The sea was as calm as an inland lake and lazy waves were breaking feebly. My deaf, manic-depressive wife was hanging from her crutches with the full weight of her six-foot body, her blond hair on her shoulders like a Dürer teen-ager. ("Six foot?" said my thin aunt among the golden tulips. "Six foot!" and plucked a dry flower. "But she looks like a Valkyrie," I said while my aunt smiled at her garden.)

My deaf, manic-depressive wife's back was turned to me and she looked out over the calm ocean while I read your letter secretly and while the clasp of her dress came undone to expose her back, red-brown like wine.

"I feel the need to confess to an impersonal and reasonably distinguished person." (Again that word "reasonably.")

"Fine. My friend C says I look as though I'm going to be very fertile. I remind her of a rich piece of earth with pools of water. I showed her a drawing of shining, lustrous loquats, big ones and little ones, and C said that's just like you, that's just like you — it's very fertile.

"Does that shed any light on your little pen friend?"

It had suddenly gone dark and the sea was black and the waves had lost their sluggishness. My deaf, manic-depressive wife's body shuddered and I thought: Emotion or cold? Is she telepathically linked with me? Has she at this moment realized something?

"Are you very busy, Mr. Y? Are you writing now? What does your wife look like?"

And my deaf, manic-depressive wife's body shook and shuddered and she swung like a pendulum on her crutches until I felt my heart would break with compassion. Impulsively I stood up, ready to do anything, and then over her shoulder I saw our reflection in the window (that's what she had been looking at all that time) — first her face, twisted in an uncontrollable fit of laughter, and then my own, miserable with anxiety.

"I wish you could see yourself," said my deaf, manic-depressive wife as she spun herself around lightly on her crutches so that I could look straight into her face, into the blue eyes filled with frenzied contempt. "I wish you could see yourself! Look at your hair! Your tie! And those manuscripts in your hand! Will you never get enough of literature?"

While she summoned the servants to lay the table, while

she warned me not to drink too much (the daughter of the goddamn drunken Swartland butcher), I finished reading your letter: "Don't write me something horrid like: 'I'd rather you found yourself another friend to write to.' A letter from you would delight me. It would make my tedious days bearable. (And I choke in the dust of my days.)"

Underneath was a drawing with this caption: "This is a drawing of my heart to bring me a little closer to you."

And then her name: "X."

And a postscript: "Last night I betrayed my own grandfather. I told a girl he's my great-grandfather."

And suddenly I found that funny and it was as if I grasped something of my deaf, manic-depressive wife's fit of laughter, because I started laughing like her and it seemed at once as if we were all twenty-five years younger and who ever forgets the things one laughed about twenty-five years ago?

But my Russian was not laughing, she looked at me the way my thin, consumptive aunt used to, and she was faintly amused and she pressed me lightly against her while her thoughts strayed among the trees and the sun in the park and I could see that she felt completely safe. I am Gemini the twin ("I am Taurus the bull. Take care, Mr. Y!") and the discord of innocence struggling with maturity and in the discord lies my futility, and callousness and cruelty, which you, Miss X, in your teen-age sensitivity, describe as treacherousness, and you, my dear Russian, as fear of being hemmed in. "And did you ever write back to her?" she asked. Yet when I said yes, she naturally did not know the whole truth: that in our letters a kind of projected identification takes place, that in this case I am forced to play the part of the father-lover, and that this role is cut out for all 44-year-olds who also "choke in the dust of their days."

Is it that a certain safety lies in complexity or is it that complexity brings one closer to one's middle-aged concept of existence? But I told her about the Russian in the letter I wrote one night by the sea when my deaf, manic-depressive wife was paying her decrepit, senile butcher-father a sentimental visit. I wrote to her as she wrote to me, and I confessed to her as she confessed to me. I told her about the evening when I met my Russian for the first time.

It was at one of those Italian places, Miss X, where Gino tries to make up for his inferior cannelloni by playing his guitar and encouraging his guests to join in, and by cramming his place impossibly full, and by illuminating the checked tablecloths with candles stuck in bottles, and by creating an atmosphere of Bohemian indigence for upper-class visitors in search of romance and escape. In my party there was an 18-year-old with hair to her shoulders surrounding her sharp little face (Is it possible that she looks like you, Miss X?) and then she started crying because of all that red wine and grief for the incomprehensibility of life while the red wine flowed freely and Gino played "Otchitshernya." A few Spanish dancers from the ballet school started dancing, we were all feeling flamenco, and then I noticed the lovely Russian before me, her yellow eyes dark with fond recollections while an elegant man waged his professional campaign of love against her with words and fondling gestures. And I saw her husband, the Cossack, big as a lion, with a lion's rage in his

16

eyes, with a rage which blazed up until he suddenly leapt to his feet and snatched the guitar from Gino's hands, and sang and danced until everyone around him sang and danced and shared his wild transport and lifted him onto a table where he accompanied his Slavic lament with the chingling of his guitar until the intruder freed his Russian wife and I, innocuous male, was left at the table alone with the crying teen-ager and the silent Russian. The melancholy of the Russian and the melancholy of the crying teen-ager while we drank red wine and the lights began to dance and the evening became chaotic and everything whirled in circles and whirled until somewhere in Gino's chamber of escape the melancholy Russian and I became entangled in each other's arms and kissed each other. The first kiss of many to come witout reason, warning, sense or end, while her husband danced his dance of death.

Can you comprehend any of this, Miss X? Do you comprehend why the crying teen-ager was knocked down and killed by the truck the following morning on her way to confess to her priest? And why my life and the life of my Russian were interwoven with her husband's dance of death and the death of the teen-ager?

What is your name, Miss X? What do you look like? Why are you writing to me and why am I writing back? Shall I find a name for you? You are one of those lovely evil little angels from a Swiss finishing school who play with life. Your name is Regina Outre-mer. That's my name for you.

"Mr. Y, Mr. Y, Mr. Y, dearest man, already I am in love with you. No, Mr. Y, my school is right here, behind the hill, where we used to neck on rugby fields on Friday nights after folk dancing. No, Mr. Y, it was not a finishing school, it was one of those places where white sandwiches always lay soaking in the lavs . . .

"I am an utterly deserted beach, Mr. Y, and birds twitter above me during the day and at night there are silences or monkeys in the bush that break out venomously in places . . ."

"I wish I were 18, Miss X, like you . . ."

When I was 18, my consumption-racked aunt took me to the Delmonico to see life, but in fact to spy on the officers from the H.M.S. *Voodoo*. She could give me an 18-year-old WAF in exchange for a 21-year-old RAF, because she was paying for everything. We danced "slows" and tangos and I can still see her hips under the soft dress as she leaned back in the dance of love. How bored the WAF was and how boisterous the RAF! How cheerless were my aunt and I on our way home in her Bentley as the WAF and the RAF disappeared into the darkness of a street corner with their arms around each other! Was it a Stuka or a Heinkel that immortalized one or the other of them in memoriam on a distant beach?

No, Miss X, I am glad I am not 18.

Generation and Degeneration

I AM GLAD I am no longer 18, Miss X, because when I was 18, my anima spoke to me with the voice of a woman of 44 and I was blind to the nymphs with hibiscus flowers in their hair and ballerina dresses and barefoot leaps over cannas. "What a solemn creature you are," said my consumption-racked aunt, and specially invited over Daphne with the pretty figure enclosed in a smartly tailored dress, with her lips tangerine and her blond hair over one eye like Veronica Lake's, and she played "Paper Doll" on my consumption-racked aunt's baby grand and I saw my aunt's eyes shining above the candelabra — clear as the silver, inscrutable in her painted face. She sent us into the moonlit garden where I talked to Daphne, who smelled of perfume, The Night Is Young, about Babylonian excavations until she said, "Aren't you going to kiss me?" But when I kissed her, her lips were tightly closed and it took me the whole evening to part her lips and, back in the light of the candelabra, she watched me with the wounded eyes of a violated virgin.

My consumption-racked aunt invited over Josephine, who played tennis with me for the entire afternoon and allowed me to beat her in races in the pool, and in the evening, after charades, hypnotized me toward the garden, unnoticed, where she pounced on me like a filly and flung herself backward so that I could barely keep both of us on our feet while she kissed me wetly and whispered Marie Corelli sentimentalities in my ear. With spit bubbles between her teeth how she murmured her love code in the light of the candelabra while I stained a whole handkerchief with dragon blood!

Marie, between me and my consumption-racked aunt, sat motionless in the city hall, right in front, listening to Yehudi Menuhin while I studied his fourth finger uninterruptedly and in his manner survived the evening in distinctive concentration. In the rose garden, under the invisible eyes of my consumption-racked aunt at the window beside the glimmering curtains, Rosamund, the artist, made certain shy suggestions that were alas impossible before the face of my aunt that had appeared like a half-moon at the second floor. Then there was Gina, the 44-year-old divorced trollop who could paint, and she and my aunt flashed around me in lightning conversations and I, clean as a pin and white as a sheet in my black suit, wanted to show her the moon, show her the moon in the rose garden, and then my comsumption-racked aunt interrupted our conversation behind the first rosebush with a "Hm-m, not for you, poppet" (in my ear) and twined my hand through her own until later, behind the candelabra, we made safe conversation while Gina's eyes glowed like red-hot iron.

Do you find it different, or odd, Miss X, in your teen-age existence of today that is so different from mine?

"You must learn to love before you can write," said my consumption-racked aunt on the way to the university she had picked for me. (Have I told you that my parents died when I was little, Miss X? I possess the faces of a man and a woman, two oval daguerreotypes in a locket.) "Languages and more languages," she told the rector as she drew on the cigarette in the long cigarette holder and contemptuously blew the smoke over his left shoulder, the little, fat man behind his enormous desk. "Languages, music, art and philosophy." I followed the flight of a bee along the bookcases on its way to the ceiling, whirling back right up past his two watery blue eyes to the desk where with a lightning blow of a prospectus he transformed the insect into a little spot of honey. "Astronomy, mathematics, anatomy and psychology." And my aunt flickered her eyes lazily in his direction and looked out of the window to where young men and girls strolled in the quadrangle in the spring sunlight. "Latin, Greek, German, French, Spanish . . ." She lifted her slender hands and embraced all the languages that came floating invisibly through the air. She dominated him, the fat little man, the famous rector who suddenly hated me and whose little, watery eyes started flashing lightning.

"Actually," said my consumption-racked aunt, "it would be better if you became the private secretary of a famous man." We were strolling around the old buildings, the ivy-covered walls, the babbling streams in the gutters. "Foreign service," she said, and lifted her arms to the sky. How tiny she looked, how slender and delicate and destructible! I could see my aunt fading away into nothingness; I saw her disappear into the sun, into a dimension of light.

We went walking in my uncle's wheat fields, which he had planted mainly for aesthetic pleasure, and waves of dark gold surged forward in the wind. The second-hand machine he had bought rose ogrelike above the horizon: a prehistoric monster on legs before the wheel was discovered; a grotesque spider of steel on which my uncle, smeared pitch-black, with white patches for eyes, made certain adjustments to the jigsaw puzzle of gears with the clairvoyance of a visionary. The motionless machine, the motionless laborers, the motionless point of extreme refinement. And then the pregnant moment when my uncle stepped back, issued orders, and watched his beloved monster in an agony of expectation. The Swartland heavens rumbled, a stream of grains bubbled into the bag, the farm hands danced the dance of life until the whole incomprehensible complex of machine and man receded into a motionless atavism, and the machine and man became part of the earth and ripe wheat, and my uncle, the prophet, began afresh, with the fingers of an artist, to conjure new life into the network of gears.

My aunt found a cornflower and spread herself like a flower among the wheat.

"An ear of corn is the image of Cybele," said my aunt. "A cornflower is the eyes of the maid Kore." She drew me down next to her, while my uncle forced the black monster to new life. "You must love women, poppet, because the language of love and women is rebirth and creation. Listen deep inside yourself. Listen!" And while I tried to listen deep inside myself, the spider bit me — the spider bite which gave my aunt so much pleasure.

Miss X, when I saw the Valkyrie, the daughter of the Swartland butcher, six feet tall, cold and hard as a diamond, even the thought of my aunt and the betrayal could not hold me. I was even prepared to endure the grading problems of beef and to grasp with insight the lament of all those who grow rich rapidly.

With my Swartland butcher-father I slithered in blood and found something poetic in the distribution of meat and fat for the sake of his Teutonic daughter and the limpid freshness of her blue eyes against the background of red carcasses, neatly arranged in ranks, frozen motionless, three inches above white sawdust, even the half-formed drops of blood iced hard as rock. Our wedding, Miss X, was a triumph of fascism over democratic acquiescence.

Our wedding nights on our honeymoon paid for by her father, in family hotels and other large-scale investments on beaches, in suites with black bathrooms, chrome lounges and four-sided views of the sea and seascapes, were something for which my consumption-racked aunt and her inspired husband, my uncle, had not prepared me. Gauleiters peered over my shoulder; the breasts of Brunhild were mounds in the snow; the sex act was a ski run at seventy miles an hour; the orgasm was a careening fury while one tried in vain to snowplow and disappeared pellmell into a wall of snow. And on the wall of snow, which had suddenly gone soft, drops of blood formed (and what is lovelier than red blood against white snow?).

She was lovely, my Valkyrie, and what, again, is more impressive than a swan-goddess of 18? Her six-foot, teenage body glowed rosily through the transparent negligee and I recalled the outline of a mountain peak one morning in Innsbruck. On the beaches, tanned brown, her blond hair windblown, she was the spring virgin of desire for all the athletic, suntanned men who saw themselves as the Siegfrieds in a twentieth-century *Nibelungenlied*. I heard Wagnerian music, Valkyries flew through the heavens and trombones played the prelude to the third act. There were fourteen days of Aryan pleasure of which my consumption-racked aunt had not told me. And there was moving into the new house in the suburbs — bought and paid for by Pa-Pa-a-a ("Were you good to my daughter?" — with incestuous envy). There was buying the silk curtains for our bedroom; black embuia for the other rooms; monstrous fridges for all the meat from the Swartland; a walnut radio-phonograph; and green marble for a green bathroom in which my beloved spent her days like a mermaid. There was never dust in the house; no pieces of furniture that did not form part of an exact square; no kitsch that was not geometrically arranged. My beloved wore herself out, formidably piquant in the little flowered apron that aroused a sort of fetishism in me which she warded off with Afrikaner purity. She wore herself out, my beloved, in her baroque castle which she furnished and sterilized quite as severely, neatly and spotlessly as her father his Germanic butchery.

We battled for three years, an olympiad in which several records were broken and fine soul mechanisms were destroyed to meet the enormous expectations of the butcher-father. (Many an intimate discussion, with the spring virgin pale in her period, with myself red with embarrassment before the flashing blue eyes.) There were interviews and examinations, at the paid command of her father of the heavy eyebrows, with an entire register of gynecologists: specialists as thorough and accurate as my new father in his own profession. And time and again, alas, the finger of indictment pointed at my lovely Brynhild, pricked by the thorn of Odin.

When finally everything had been irrefutably proved, my father-in-law looked at me in fury to explain to me all that I already knew — and I pitied him in that measure one always pities men of action who are frustrated in the end because of shortcomings which can only be attributed to themselves and their brood.

"In the animal world, Y," he told me while, hairy paws clasped together, he leaned back comfortably in a Morris chair he had paid for himself, "there are a number of animals, usually of the female gender, even from the best stud, which cannot reproduce."

He accepted the drink I had offered him without perceptible sympathy.

"They are the loveliest animals: the fattest cows, the most perfect ewes."

He took a swig from the glass that I had poured with a heavy hand and meditated a moment before continuing.

"We, as butchers, are often placed in a position to buy such animals for slaughter purposes . . ."

It was as if a certain, unknown emotion overwhelmed him. He looked past me, at the embuia furniture, the kitsch and vulgar symmetry so dear to him, and he seemed to take fresh courage. His voice was louder, stronger.

"They are destined for the abattoirs, but in these cases we pay the highest prices per pound. If the market is twenty-five cents, we do not hesitate to pay twenty-seven. They are worth it — even if we pay a cent or two more for sentiment."

He accepted another drink, even more strongly spiced in a sympathy which I could only show with a heavier hand.

"Is there a more slandered profession? '. . . do we not bleed?' "

He looked at me with Aryan eyes, but I was instantly filled with love and compassion for my Swartland butcher-father and his Shakespeare from the days of a farm school: square and trim, among clover and buttercups.

He noticed the compassion — the merchant, orientated to public appraisal.

"I am pleased you understand," he said, and placed a heavy, hairy, soft paw on my arm. That was the first and last gesture of tenderness and emotion evinced by my butcher-father toward someone not good at sport or successful in business.

He first emptied his glass and then he said: "We have a name for those animals. Any breeder could tell you. We call them queens."

And at that moment my spring wife came in, breathlessly lovely in her nonpregnancy, a model of glowing Germanic womanhood, icily attractive as the snow that longed for her, her face snow-white as the frost into which her invisible blood seeps.

And my butcher-father and I drank simpatico to something which neither of us could comprehend: he to sterility, for that was his profession; I to sterility, for that was my destiny.

"Mr. Y, Mr. Y, Mr. Y. You are magenta-pink and Bordeaux-red. I fear a purple in your composition. There is something treacherous in the purple. You like women to be crisp and sweet like ripe watermelon. Dangerously ripe. Just before they turn poisonously sweet. Your flowers are cannas, orange cannas, and your anima is a white lily.

"That frightens me, that combination of cannas and a white lily. I am a visual type, Mr. Y."

Was my Russian dangerously ripe? I looked at her with her kohl-covered eyelids, the untidy eyelashes, and her mouth, magenta-pink, moist from my kisses, and for the first time I noticed the only flowering corner in the neglected park, laid out in the form of a triangle by the gardener who later went to work in Welgevonden: a triangle of luxuriant, gay orange cannas.

But is my anima a white lily? When I was eighteen, and I projected the experience of the repressed Eros, it was onto my consumption-racked aunt. Today (still immature according to my friend the homosexual architect of my cottage by the sea) I am still in search of women who will carry my anima value, powerless to reconcile myself with the feminine quality in myself, searching still, but now for younger and prettier girls.

"If that is so, then you, Miss X, you are my white lily."

"Mr. Y, Mr. Y, Mr. Y. My eyes are limitlessly empty, my

27

body is not part of me, it washes dim and pale onto many beaches that are cold."

"Mr. Y, forgive me my fantasies and always see me in the light of my teenhood."

"Mr. Y, your letters disturb me . . . !"

"Miss X, have you ever thought about this: why did you write to me? What are you trying to say, what do you want?"

"Mr. Y, Mr. Y, Mr. Y. I expect shells and leaves that rustle and always rustle blood-red. Look, Mr. Y, look, look, look. I'm throwing you plums, many many shiny, soft, kidney-red plums . . ."

"Mr. Y, I lean over your shoulder and very alone and very remotely I touch you lightly, only lightly, with my fingers . . ."

Like the sun in this park of my youth, Miss X, which unites two worlds in the flashes between the leaves, which touches me sharply with memories and shocks me fleetingly with the passing moment, with the Cossack in contrapuntal reality in the encroaching future, and with the eyes of my crippled, deaf, manic-depressive wife fixed on me as I read your letters between my manuscripts.

"I like you because you are cruel," said my fiery Russian. "I like you because you have a cold, remote core; I like you because you can dominate me with the strength of your remoteness," unaware of her husband, the Cossack, on his vengeful journey, and his army of two in the tranquil, sunny park. An edelweiss park, where child heroes fought without a scratch against the tyrants and enemies of their youth and died valiantly with a lusty flow of imaginary blood.

"I think you are fine and soft, Mr. Y, and very scared."

And there is a drawing of her left hand with the image of a man on it — a man with wings like Hermes without a message from the gods.

"You will write," said my Valkyrie wife with a blue apron around her full waist, "and you will become one of the most famous writers," while she fried pork sausages and chips in the pan, "and you will . . ." Speechless, with the pan in the air, full of crackling little pork noises — a gesture against the future, a triumph over her barrenness by means of her husband's spiritual fertility . . .

"I don't understand one word you write," said the Swartland butcher-father. "Do your books sell well?"

Not too well, but there is a certain formula and the formula is like his butchery: one develops a cunning — an inflated package to inflate a lower-grade product. My butcher-father and I suddenly had a better understanding of each other and gradually developed a fondness for each other.

"Now that's something to get one's teeth into!" said my butcher-father as the sales improved.

"That's not what I meant," said my consumption-racked aunt on her gracious deathbed, before she ordered me to leave. My consumption-racked aunt within her own limitations.

According to what image of what bygone civilization did she raise me? If you were as old as I, you might have possibly been asked to grasp something of all this, but it would be an impossible task to explain it all to you now. When I returned from Europe, she was on the quay at three-thirty in the morning and I was asleep in the cabin;

and there I saw her, covered with frills and feathers, an apparition of autumn, an autumn leaf against the green, a speck through the porthole against the background of a gray waterfall on the mountain. I wiped the sleep from my eyes, I wiped Europe from my eyes, the better to see my aunt, and my heart was full to tell her everything I had experienced and endured — for the first time in my life, to communicate something to someone, something indescribable. How exhilarating the meeting was; with what disdain she kept the customs man off my presents for her; how eagerly she wanted to see her own world in my eyes! She kissed me like a lover, her lips moist, and there was a timid touch of her tongue which she immediately withdrew and used avidly for questions and more questions. And then it became clear to me that my Paris was not hers: the air of respectability of her bistro on the right bank against the slightly extravagant dissipation of my *rhumerie* on the left bank — just as *your* Paris will also be, Miss X, different from mine.

But that's when I realized, Miss X, how we all project ourselves upon each other in roles with which we identify ourselves, and how we constantly seek the lost half in others, and how we try to understand that invisible, incomprehensible, disturbing something in ourselves, to give it an image, to force the mute image in ourselves to communicate. How incomprehensible the bold youth was to his 44-year-old aunt; how wise and excitingly complex the aunt was to the unripe 18-year-old youth! How the two of us, in projection, in the sunny park, in the wheat fields, in my uncle's cellars, drunk on his wine, tried to comprehend something about ourselves! But the final result was always, in the hangover, in the moment of realization, a sad disillusionment: that she could not be the bearer and I could not be the bearer of the unformed truths which we sought in each other. My consumption-racked aunt and I were equally unripe and immature: I was the young god, Attis, castrated in a pine tree; she was a Cybele who could not grasp the meaning of her orgies.

"Miss X, it seems that I am now in the role of my consumption-racked aunt toward you. You are a dryad, a nymph, can I ever understand you, and what are we going to do?"

"Mr. Y, the wise man will know. He is wise and he will know."

"That's what I mean, Miss X, that's exactly what I mean . . ."

"I feel safe with you, Mr. Y. I no longer look at you; I see through your eyes . . ."

"But that's wrong, Miss X. That's wrong. You must seek within yourself, and in yourself, try to find what you are seeking."

"I am young, Mr. Y. I am young and I understand so very little. But I kiss your hands, Mr. Y, Mr. Y, Mr. Y. Can you feel my breath on your cheek? I wish I could sleep with you tonight."

"Then I shall simply have to coddle you, and give you the temporary protection, Miss X, that you seek in me . . ."

"I wish I could sleep with you," said the Russian in the sunny park, "because I am 44 and this is my first real love and the days are flying by and will you like me when I am old?"

What will happen when we are old? The little old man and the little old woman there among the flowers are zombies. The anima and the animus speak a language incomprehensible to all the old people who seek a child's paradise here in this Victorian park. The halcyon's feather has blown away; Philemon is no more than a shadow among the trees.

"You will not like me," said the Russian. She closed her eyes, and I saw the kohl on her eyelids and the fine wrinkles around her eyes that were still attractive. My Russian showed her lovely leg to me, and she rolled her pelvis beneath the expensive dress, because time is passing, time is passing, and all that remains is sadness for those fleet-footed lost seconds that leave, at every moment, a reminder of some wasted opportunity: the lightning flash of an inspiration that came too late, the lost point of intersection of like emotions, the aftereffects of a lost ecstasy which one can later re-create only in a sterile dream of wish fulfillment.

I am a product of my consumption-racked aunt, Miss X. Faced with you and the Russian, I also appreciate the danger of my own limitations, because we are interwoven, and our only salvation lies in the possibility that I, the hack, can find a certain degree of insight. I belong to the in-between generation, Miss X, and my longing is for an in-between world, and, who knows, perhaps the answer lies with those of us who can reconcile the answers of two generations in an in-between world.

I kissed my Russian, I stroked her elegant leg, I let my hand rest lightly on all the places of love, and I aroused promises in her on whose fulfillment her Slavic blood would insist. And I possessed her heart because she believes that my helpless remoteness is the cruelty which she can understand, because she does not know the checkmate of our bourgeois existence in this sunny, sterile country.

Is it possible that you know this in the nowhere land of your teen-age existence, Miss X?

I HAVE JUST HEARD that song: "I can't tell my teardrops from the rain," and I suddenly had a picture of myself, Miss X, as old as you are now, in a room behind a window in the house of my uncle who had just died, while my consumption-racked aunt stood on the lawn under a black umbrella. In the distance an avenue of blue gums telescoped toward the wheat fields; the fields of clover were lovelier than I had ever seen them; the dunes were bone-white among the proteas and heather; the thresher was the colossal skeleton of a prehistoric monster against the horizon, lying naked under the gray heaven. My consumption-racked aunt, tall and straight backed in her black dress, had just bade farewell to the hordes of funeral guests (it must have been one of the biggest funerals within living memory in the community) and all that was left was a memory of my uncle who had always tried to adapt the world to himself with the prettiest and most unlikely strain of sheep or cattle: stud animals from Scotland, Ireland, Germany and France; and plants that were unheard of in the district — everything for the heart, the eye and the imagination. And all that was now left was the landscape in its final triumph over my uncle, the gray, rainy weather possibly a gesture of mourning, and my consumption-racked aunt in black unexpectedly alone, utterly alone, except for her little nephew behind the window, who, for the first time, conceived of the impermanence of everything and who wept with nature for a world which had passed away and would never return again. It was a moment of intense awareness for the youth in whose heart one tragic novel after another was born in a moment — a moment of joy even in the living concept of life's elements revealed to him so dramatically. Then his aunt returned with the black umbrella held ever so high above her head, streams of water on every side of her, mascara streaks over her face, her dress like a shroud around her body. And he wept with the rain for his dead uncle, his dazed aunt and the utopian days that were also dead for always and always. He saw her go in through the door, he saw her in the hallway and he prepared himself to hold his arms open to her so that in her grief she would find refuge and comfort with him. He saw her consumption-racked figure, her back turned to him, her weary face in the passage mirror and he heard her cry: "Je-e-e-s-u-s!" He ran to her, but she had already gone into her room and he had to wait long and anxiously at the locked door before she would appear again, freshly made up and calm as ice, and in the years to follow he often wondered whether she had called her Maker to witness for her sorrow or her battered appearance.

I must tell you something, Miss X, so that you will also be able to imagine my nowhere lands.

The following morning my aunt and I set fire to the prehistoric monster. (A just requital because the steel beast had been the cause of my uncle's death. My uncle had been stretched out under the belly of his monster when one of the steel legs gave way and she, the female spider, had sunk down upon him in a love embrace and crushed him into the unrecognizable being that is her self.) My

35

consumption-racked aunt (in her autumn attire once more) and I set fire to the monstrosity after the funeral but it took a whole box of matches before anything caught on fire — there was so much steel and so much cast iron and so little wood. But my aunt was not satisfied and took up a sledgehammer in her assault upon the presence of the monster, and the monster fought back with steel splinters which made a neat little cut on her arm through her silk blouse, from which the blood, the scant blood of my aunt, flowed with all the irrepressibility of her vast spirit.

We attacked the farm with the same daring with which we had attacked the monster, Miss X. My consumptive aunt and I. We assaulted the farm with all the impractical enthusiasm we jointly possessed. Within a year we had achieved what it took my deceased uncle a whole lifetime to accomplish in his aestheticism. We created a picturesque, unproductive, divine, nature-bound piece of earth that left the new owner with an idiotic feeling of impossibility. And then my aunt and I set out on our travels through her world which were to end with my marriage with the Valkyrie, who — and I realize it now for the first time — forced my aunt for the last time in her life to call her Maker to witness for the death with which He destroys all nowhere lands.

"Are you happy?" my consumption-racked aunt asked me in a whisper, years after the butcher wedding, reposing in my Swartland father's Morris chair into which she disappeared slenderly while my embittered, plump swan-wife carried in cakes and espresso coffee.

"Yes," I said at that stage, although my spring wife was, strictly speaking, no longer attractive, but because she still desperately, for the sake of the Swartland tradition and for the sake of the stocky ruddy father, wanted to prove her procreative capacity by forcing her little male writer into the role of a satyr — which he, in the prime of his years, played with alacrity, unaware of the approaching shift: the crack in the ice; the tiny, barely visible hair cracks; the prelude to the horrible estrangement.

Occasionally, Miss X, like my consumption-racked aunt, I also want to call my Maker to witness for the death of our own nowhere land: the twilight world of the ice animal, the cold, passionate north — even though there was no love, even though it was no more than a Germanic Götterdämmerung of sex, with my Swartland butcher-father an enthusiastic spectator, invisible, over pale white shoulders in the darkness of the battle-scarred four-poster.

He could always inquire for news, my sturdy pioneer of the art of butchery, with the lift of an eyebrow, with a darkening in his otter eyes. And, like my consumption-racked aunt, he could also in his own right call evidence to witness the end of his nowhere land when he died of heart failure (where was his heart?) with his hopes yet unfulfilled.

I must tell you, because you must know, Miss X, of my swan-wife, who, after the death of her father, was suddenly left alone with herself, because you must have knowledge of the nowhere lands and the dew-drop existence of nowhere lands. Her six-foot body could take that slight robustness, because the Valkyrie was full of glowing life (in contrast with the emaciated body of my consumption-racked aunt). Her barrenness, years before the discovery of the Pill, gave her an unexpected feeling of freedom. One unmarked day she looked at her husband with limpid blue eyes, pure and calculating with a newborn comprehension, and, rid of the burden of her loved ones, she felt the powerful source of her Amazon existence: six feet of health, energy and vitality. The first thing she asked him was: What are you doing? The hours of frustration and adolescent offerings were not enough. Why don't you *work?* Work for the heroic woman was a certain dynamism in several forms: physically, or through the reality of recognized corporate organizations. If you love me you must *love* me, and that meant: heroic love according to the romantic ideals of love stories she had read; satisfying, caressive formulae in women's magazines; the activeness of sports heroes and bloomingly healthy young men carefully cultivated by various provincial educational administrations — the whole product of positive conditioning to which my Valkyrie was subject in a young and vital country.

That was also something for which my consumption-racked aunt, for the umpteenth time, had not prepared me.

We once went to a party, Miss X, and my beloved began to bloom after her winter sleep as only an Afrikaner girl can bloom: exuberant, gay, companionable and full of life, and everyone was there, the sons and daughters of active fathers who had attained the upper-middle-class bracket. And the barbecue and the wine and the dancing on the plot as big as a farm was something to dream about: red lanterns among the trees (red lights have a degrading significance only in Europe), horseplay intimacies when blue jokes cried to high heaven with peasant innocence, a glorious earthiness without ritual, gluttony in the sinless mask of unbounded nature (like Bushmen and Bantu at the slaughter of kudu and ox), beer, barbecued meat and brandy where the cold north and warm south came together sensually and senselessly while the athletic young man and the hardworking, lascivious housewife transformed the rumble of a drunken discussion into the melody of a successful party. "This party's *moving!*" cried my elated host, and, provided one exercises a little care and avoids being caught up in the deep discussions of decrepits about profound generalities, one always has the prospect of that blushing child by the barbecue grills who will regale one with the silences of her knowledge — and possibly delight one with the endowments of her youth.

My Valkyrie, Miss X, was the life and soul of the gathering. Does it matter when or where it was? Her laughter repeatedly rang out above the rest; she was in complete harmony with the barbecue; her figure was a challenge to the sportsmen and athletes who mumbled their profundities to her in the Marlon Brando style. It was an enormously successful evening, Miss X, and it was the evening I lost my Valkyrie wife. The party had reached its chaotic climax: all around, couples appeared and disappeared among the trees like phantoms. Delivered at last from the Oom, the popular farmer who had expounded his point of view to be discussed at the coming national agricultural congress to me, I started looking for my Valkyrie, for her six-foot body and for her limpid blue eyes that were part of our nowhere land. But all I encountered was the beatific lingering that marks the end: the shoulder-slapping, the jovial greetings and all the friendly gestures through which utter insensibility jeers outwardly. I looked for her in rooms, in lavs, in light and dark corners, among the maids in the kitchen, satiated among the left-over meat, and even in the pantry, where I took a cold beer from the fridge to bolster my courage. The bourgeois, suburban rich man's house all at once became a frightful threat. I hated my happy host and hostess who, with their arms around their guests, were lapping the last drops of pleasure from their party. I became involved in their company and precious moments were lost. I dragged myself free from their hospitality and I ranged alone over lawns and past rose trees that giggled and then at last I found her: correct, sedate, apparently courteously interested in a young man, well built like herself, innocent in the light of the red lantern where they were eating asparagus. My Valkyrie wife, with the green stains of dead insects and dried foliage on her back, and her escort, with the nice eyes in which he could barely disguise sympathy and contempt as he looked at me in a friendly way.

You must try to conceive of these nowhere lands, Miss X — or perhaps you know them: the frantic round from one party to another that later, despite the different and even interesting types of people, develops into a sort of sameness. And the odd thing is, Miss X, that one becomes used to it; one eventually cannot do without it, even though one hates one's own repetitions and the endless repetition of coming and going, laughing and enjoying, and a synthetic world which provides an undeviating recipe for entertainment and escape. But it seemed my Valkyrie wife thrived in these circumstances: she lost just enough weight to make her prettier; she devoted more attention to herself; and with the aid of cosmetics and *Vogue* she achieved the sort of appearance that would make her attractive to all men in spite of the fact that her mind was sealed in a lacquered cocoon and her heart wrapped in a shroud of durable corsetry. I lost my Valkyrie wife that first evening forever and could never find her again in that sterile world in which she was trying to escape her own sterility, and my life consisted of a fascinated dreamlike search among red lights, music, laughter and lightning sex in the midst of twentieth-century instant baroque.

Did you know that all writers, even hacks, are myopic, Miss X? That also means that they can barely see in the dark — and that the search for my snow queen was a descent into hell in the pleasure world where colored lights are intended to blunt one's sharpness of vision and to make emotional awareness come alive with a woolly rhythm very like the flights of feeling of drugged saxophonists. I searched for her in sorrow, Miss X, because I have the mercy of someone who knows the nature of nowhere lands. Sometimes I could see beyond the masks (both real and unreal) the grin of the masked god; sometimes I could sense the tragedy; sometimes I could laugh through the mask of a clown at myself and at everyone else.

It is difficult to extricate oneself from the clutches of clouds, and how can I relate the sequence of events of that particular evening lucidly and simply, even though disasters are simple and lucid like matter-of-fact reports in newspapers?

It was a magnificent evening in terms of the pleasure world: it was as if all middle-class housewives had united their meager powers of imagination and, in the union, had achieved something greater than the sum total of their knowledge. It was as if Nature itself had entered into the game for all of us: the stars and the black sky formed a limitless vault; the barbecue fires a Wodan forge; the goddess of love in her scanty garment was present in person among the women, who in their turn also became living archetypes — an orgy of lust in a suburban garden. I could scarcely see her, my brilliant wife, in the clasp of someone I recognized at once as the great god of nature, out to take vengeance on the depraved feminine mystique, in his wrath aroused by the perversion of his mysteries.

I looked at her, I talked to her, but in her eyes was that blue light of madness that is his color. She looked past me; she looked over my shoulder and her beatified insanity streaked out toward the obscure gloom beyond the barbecue fires. Something had happened beneath the surface and I was utterly powerless.

I looked at her, my icy wife, in the embrace of the warm god who was going to destroy her because she was cold and sterile. I tried to find words and all I could scrape up was commonplace chatter while she disappeared under my eyes.

There is death in the air, my divine hostess, right in the middle of your heavenly party, and I am trying, myopically, to find an immediate truth that will immunize us both, my Valkyrie wife and I, against death. (My hostess, the upper-middle-class peasant, unreceptive to complex suffering, looks quizzically at me.) I am looking for something like your instant coffee, dearest hostess, after all that wine and drink — and how can I improve on your instant coffee even though I really need something else that takes time and devotion?

That's the nature of foggy parties: certain truths lie locked up in the unreality around one; one has a glimpse of the truth and then everything is lost. I looked into the eyes of my Teutonic wife, I grasped something and I lost her for the hundredth time in the bustle. I found her corpse in an overturned Karmann Ghia.

No, it was not a corpse. She would never walk without crutches again, but she was not a corpse — even though it looked that way; the six-foot broken body at the cross-roads to an unknown destination, behind a Karoobush, not quite a mile from the Coney Island house. He should have been killed, the stunned athletic guest in his dinner jacket, bleeding slightly from a light wound on the temple.

He had guts, the athlete and cricket player: he called the doctor (his hands bleeding); he looked me squarely in the eye. He was a perfect gentleman. (And we were all gentlemen for the sake of propriety — that evening when my Valkyrie wife was carried to the ambulance on a stretcher.)

That was the end of the nowhere land, Miss X.

Nowhere land is not always a pretty land. Nowhere lands end: poof!

Reproaches and rumors lasted a day or two.

After that it would have been unseemly and in bad taste; moreover, unnecessary when a sacrifice had already been made.

Blade Wounds

Miss X drew a black and red yin-yang symbol for me. ("Do you know it, Mr. Y?") And, by way of an answer to her cosmic gesture, I took a blade and flicked open my wrist between the veins so that a few drops of blood dropped onto the letter I was writing her. ("Is it a mandala, Miss X?") The blood stained the paper with the red I know she loves, but the following morning, and the morning after that, the blood turned black as wood and at once I saw this as a disturbing sign that true communication is impossible. ("It's a Chinese symbol, Mr. Y, in which the black and red are immiscibly mingled.") The wound took a long time to heal and the tiny cut left a mark on my skin which is still there — a white blaze among the brown and black liver spots — and I warned her not to try it, because I could visualize her white wrist with the veins blue upon it.

She sent me a drawing of a seahorse ("Take good care of it, Mr. Y — I'm very attached to him") and she sent me a drawing of five colorful shells which caught the sharp eye of my deaf, manic-depressive wife. "Shells? Shells?" she said. "Who has ever heard of colored shells?" And she rocked back and forth jeering on her crutches with her long, bony finger, against the background of the still, blue sea, pointing at the "manuscript."

My Russian gave me a talisman of coral, ice-cold against my hand, as big as a fifty-cent piece, to wear next to my heart for her sake, for good luck and fortune. We kissed each other under the cork oak; her lips were wide and warm and children were playing among the cannas in the distance on the grass-green grass, and then she walked away, aware of my eyes unwavering upon her, in a self-conscious exit through the trellised gates of my consumption-racked aunt's park. She walked with restrained grace, her head slightly crooked with concentration: a picture for me that she consciously created in that isolated moment in the midst of our dying years.

"I like roses, Mr. Y. Water is also important, but only at night. During the day water is only beautiful for reflections. I was sitting on a smooth, bone-white, sand-white tree stump that had washed ashore, warm and smooth, and pools of water mirrored reflections of the tree stump . . ."

"There is a sweet pain in my heart, Mr. Y. But I want to play with paper dolls and eat *must-rusks*. Mr. Y, Mr. Y, Mr. Y, what will become of us? I take Libriums to calm my tattered nerves."

She sent me plum leaves, nasturtiums, beach grass, a piece of cloth from the shirt she was wearing, hairs from her arms, the imprint of her lips in Max Factor Pink Frost, and a streak of Charles of the Ritz mascara, "waterproof, tearproof, rainproof, bathproof, swimproof . . ."

"Heaven alone knows what will happen to us, Miss X."

Behind the ravaged face of my wife I saw the sea and the waves that are more than the bare product of wind and current. I saw a streetlight, a woman flashing by in an S.S. Jaguar, and in the distance the silver trees among which Princess Ira von Liebenstein, like a restless ghost, is searching for a world which no longer exists. My deaf, manic-depressive wife's voice rang hard and incessant, like the voice of all deaf people, as she wailed her frustrations against a world she can hardly hear, but can see with keen bitterness. The past was flowing further and further away through the tunnel that was her mouth; her voice was a somber trumpeting of gloom.

"You are Yugoslavia against the Russia of my Russian, Miss X."

"I don't begrudge you your Russian, Mr. Y."

What will become of us, Miss X? You grow older daily; daily I grow younger and more vulnerable as my power of perception increases.

She sent me a drop of her blood, black as my own after a day, and she told me her dream:

I dreamed I was at school again in a little room that leads into a big studio and there was no one, it was very still, and behind me through the giant windows shone a yellow light that made the whole room glow (always these glowing rooms in my dreams) and a beautiful pink vase shattered into a thousand pieces. I collected the pieces of glass and pressed them tightly together until they fitted like a jigsaw puzzle while my thumbs bled just where they join the hands. I felt no pain in the midst of all that blood. It spilled everywhere, my quick-flowing blood, and I could hear myself crying as I walked toward the man who awaited me in the studio — I cried, and, as far as I walked, I saw only blood flowing and I wanted to go to him and throw my arms around his neck, which was suddenly covered with blood, because I knew the blood would stop as soon as I reached him. And then I looked up, and I saw the man was you.

You are projecting an impersonal sexual instinct upon me, the hack, Miss X. Shall I pretend to be Pan? Shall I return the cruelty for which you secretly long? Let me tell you about blade wounds.

My Swartland butcher-father, surrounded by blood throughout his life, died bloodlessly: pale, blue and whole. My consumption-racked aunt, in the valley of death of her Seconals, had to suffer the bloody, razor-keen knife of a post-mortem. (The nurse was right: she went in silence while my Swartland butcher-father rattled a full-throated protest.) Let us pronounce judgment together, Miss X, on my Swartland butcher-father and my consumption-racked aunt: a judgment on him for his life but not for his death; a judgment on her for her death but not for her life.

"Mr. Y, Mr. Y, Mr. Y, you disturb me. I don't like you like this. I see you as an angel with elusive timid eyes and a soft, soft voice."

I looked into my Russian's eyes in which thousands of years of existence glittered hard as rock beyond the shimmer of love. My Russian and I in the park that my consumption-racked aunt had bequeathed us from her own urbane world. We were meeting there regularly, we knew every corner and tree, blade of grass and monument — each a witness of forbidden love. We knew it in the moonlit nights of our imagining that transformed the banality of physical love into the wizardry of flickering silver among the leaves; we knew it in the red-fire blaze of the sun when all was still and deserted and only the impersonal eyes of the flat-dwellers on high awaited any perceptible decadence. It was a Gothic park in which my Russian and I found ourselves. It was, in the center of the city, something of two worlds: a place of impossible meeting,

47

like 18 and 44; and my Swartland butcher-father and my consumption-racked aunt; and the Teutonic north and Mediterranean south; and the spiritual incompatibility of a man and a woman of the same age. A Gothic park of opposites: the severe, Gothic elongation, which is a form of distortion, against the horizontal plane of romantic love, which is a form of escape; the park of contrasts in which each of us reaches, like a monolith, not only toward heaven, but also to seek our counterimage in the earth.

My Russian told me of her strange youth in a country that is foreign to me: all those blade wounds upon all those children throughout the world who grew into the scarred adults that inhabit this new, illimitable world. She told me of a black train through white snow, the coffin trucks sealed by ice; the heaped bodies lukewarm and damp in the dark; the forest on the mountain like the mane on a wolf's back; the woodcutter's house with its light falling through the window while rough hands became entangled in her maiden hair among rags — all those silent outrages among the lowing of human suffering while the train pounded through the immeasurable desert of snow. She told me, in the sunny park, Miss X, of cannibalistic hunger and cats and dogs that showed their friendship to man in terms of warm blood and warm flesh. She told me of a bayonet three inches from her face through the sides of a crate that was simultaneously her hiding place and her prison; of morphine to still her childish crying; of a flaming sun above an iron truck forgotten on a siding — all that suffering and all those blade wounds on that neglected little scamp with the ragged hair, her apple breasts bruised, and an indecent cunning in her eyes. I could not recognize the scamp in the ripe, well-groomed woman in my consumption-racked aunt's park, and yet they had a whole world in common: Prokofiev's music and the ballet that my consumptive aunt enjoyed on Cook's tours and in gracious lounges, which my Russian (still a little girl who gathered blackberries in black forests) paid for in the blood of her blade wounds.

Do you understand why my Russian is impatient, Miss X, and why she hates the passing years, and the wistfulness of your teenhood, and my remoteness which she still sees as cruelty?

We prey on each other like wild animals, Miss X. We are once more living in my Russian's world. Even though you grew up exchanging friendly kisses in flower-filled suburbia, the wolves still slink around soundlessly at night between swimming pools, shrubs and nasturtiums over bowling-green lawns.

You pray in vain to Purah, Miss X, with the help of your Libriums. Like my Russian, you must realize that you live always between the divine and the temporal and that, in the midst of your peaceful middle-class existence, you fight an unbroken battle in your monthly tides between life and death. You are my anima, Miss X, as you yourself said, but you are also my ego (we are irrevocably interwoven) *inter bona et mala* . . .

I send you the red blood (that has now turned black) as the blood of the mediator: the black and the red blood as a *matrimonium* or *conjunctio.* I am that Hermes you drew; I am Hermes Trismegistos the orphan, the color of your cannas, the individual who can still glow in the dark, the wine-colored symbol that I radiate for my loved ones: my

Russian, my nymph, my deaf, manic-depressive wife and my consumption-racked aunt who left this bloody park for us all.

For the second time I slashed open my wrist and I sent Miss X my canna-colored blood — a red-black splash on the paper — and I struggled for months with the wound that would not heal: a wound of penance and atonement.

I DREW A CASTLE haunted by Laura for Miss X.

I can hear the rustling of her dress in the passage, her voice raised above the dunes in a lament; I see her specter, on our way to the green sea, among the specters of pale sailors beside the unknown captain's grave at the crossroads, through the window of the Whippet driven by my merry uncle, years ago, with my consumption-racked aunt next to him, surrounded by food baskets and His Master's Voice records — bouncing up and down, across traverses, sliding from left to right through the white sand on the road to Witsand, among bonteboks and ostriches, in the howling wind through the murky gray mist to our mystic destination in candlelit rooms where the sea would come sailing toward us menacingly over moonsilver dapples with the blood-chilling screams of the captain and his men, and then recede smudgily with a funereal chant in the sweet voice of Laura, my ghost beloved.

At night the dust ranged around the captain's grave; during the day everything was still and we caught crabs in the shadow of the derelict wreck of his ship; a slim Viking girl (a descendant of the deceased captain?), her golden hair over her shoulders, her limbs brown and supple as a young boy's, playfully caught a deep-sea monster and tried my courage with the creature's claws that drew blood from my soft skin. I saw my consumption-racked aunt, lightly intoxicated with champagne, who was trying me wordlessly in her own way, lying to one side under a beach umbrella next to my limply dozing uncle, unaware of the crashes of lightning on the sunny beach. I died of terror motionlessly — I died fearlessly without moving for the sake of two worlds. I followed my Nordic boy-girl throughout the day: into caves where we all smelled a dangerous decay (the sperm of forbidden love); in treasure hunts over dunes; in silent adoration where suntanned bodies dappled and teased beneath a red-black sun; in the purple glow of dusk while my Brynhild (the murderess) froze into silhouette against the horizon on the immobile wreck, deserted in the deceptive calm of low tide.

"She's the daughter of a butcher," said my consumption-racked aunt, hopelessly intoxicated with champagne and holidays, under the rainbow lights of the rococo hotel, before she moved into the rhythm of the late thirties in the arms of a man sporting a blazer, white trousers and a Valentino spit curl.

I surprised my aunt as I had often surprised myself in my dreams: when I opened the door, I saw a room where everything was unintelligible. "Careful, poppet!" And I swiftly closed the door on a black nylon stocking-clad leg in the air, folded in a white sheet; portions of the human torso in unusual combination — a collusion of objects as unreal as a pantomime, where a white sail and a green light represent water, where two boots and a woman are a cat; where London looms up before my eyes behind a white milestone.

Youth is indestructible, Miss X. I closed the door on a nonfigurative image: an abstraction which puzzled me but did not leave me dissatisfied; an image utterly in accord with my own world. In those years one lives in the multiplicity of broad strokes; and you possibly have a more lucid comprehension of life and death.

Years later, when my crippled wife started going deaf and when she took out her rage against life on the hack (the little male in the harris tweed jacket who did not "work" and whom she had to support on the money left by her blessed father), I often thought back to the white beach and the elusive, cruel Valkyrie girl, half a head taller than the boys, the center of adoration, unattainable to the little boy who, on the outskirts of his group, would have traded his butterfly soul for a bare recognition of his existence. He could read meaning into her eyes resting on him for a few seconds; or when her arm touched him hotly; or when she threw a scrabbling crab down his back as he turned to stone in terror under the knowing eyes of his aunt, lightly and wistfully drunk under the beach umbrella.

The dances, Miss X; the dances on the beaches and the Christian Students' Association services and the folk dancing which symbolize the whole complexity of the Afrikaner's spiritual make-up! (My Russian found it strange and rare and incomprehensible when I tried to describe it to her in the sunny park.) Christian Students' Association services at night when the group leader in a black suit, his patent-leather shoes buried in the sand, stirred us above the wind to the religion of our ancestors, when his well-modulated voice, raised against the lament of the captain and the waves, lured us to the cosy, homely circle of family prayers, to Sunday school and middle-class exemplitude, and to Christ, not of the desert and loneliness, but of neat, shiny lounges and conference auditoriums — the valedictorian of the school, head prefect, chairman of the

53

temperance society and *victor ludorum*, who years later, in maturity, lost in the petty cycle of work, often wonders what has become of his golden key to success. Tent services at campsites along Boer beaches while lights twinkled in the distance and lay preachers glorified sin before damning it, and childish souls formulated their desolation in clichés in public confessions. With my heroine girl in the van, passionately abandoned as she abandoned herself to all the games in which she was the leader. Folk dancing in the moonlight under the approving eyes of fathers who would go fishing before sunrise the following morning, sentimental on brandy, their fat stomachs full of curry, shish kebabs and dried peaches, their foreheads platitudinous white parchments, their overtaxed hearts, rightly, meant only for pumping blood, their desires quickly quenched by the lightninglike matrons who, stiffly erect, having gluttonously tasted at all the toothsome dishes, were knitting over flowered laps as they watched my Valkyrie beloved dancing in the lead and gossiped about her father who sold third-grade meat as first-grade because of his monopoly. Real dances at the hotel under colored lights and Chinese lanterns, with strange, middle-aged wolves sitting at lonely tables, their tango-partner mustaches symmetrical, their bald heads shined with cologne, their little commercial-traveler eyes shining with faith in the products they had to sell and the by-product of their profession — to fritter away their ravaged charm on fluffy, ripe and lithe young girls bouncing to the beat of folk rock . . . No, Miss X, in those years it was not folk rock; it was the pounding rhythm of bop. And my Valkyrie was right up front, her limbs slender under the shiny silk dress, a lilting virgin beside my consumption-racked aunt, limp as a lullaby in the arms of the Valentino while my uncle at his corner table was refusing to sell three Corriedale rams to Boland farmers who had heard of him and who thought they could catch him with the bouquet of the estate wines they were pouring freely.

And the wind was blowing for a young boy who held a Germanic dream in his arms in the Paul Jones; blowing the wind and murmuring the sea, for him, while he did a series of steps to three-quarter time. Drunk as his aunt on his first forbidden beer, he heard Laura in the ecstasy of the half-turn and everything grew quiet when he went outside and, gloriously alone, looked at the waves where the phosphorescent lights came to meet his romantic thoughts in an illusion wrought by his befuddled, beer-bound brain.

The first signs of deafness in my crippled wife slipped by us all unmarked, Miss X, because she accepted the additional sentence, that she would never walk again without crutches, with a rancor that she was only able to show by silence when we comforted her, and by withdrawal when we tried to make her aware that life goes on. I looked into her rebellious eyes many times and never realized that there were also deeper pools in her shallow world — that in her extroverted existence she must have been aware of a flash of fleeting puzzles beneath the shimmering surface. What did I know of the swan when she was an ugly duckling — when she was an awkward little filly before an approaching womanly ripeness magically transformed her into a magnificent thoroughbred and made her an object of desire and lust so that never again, like others, would she feel the need to look beneath the gloss of superficiality.

Did my crippled Valkyrie, with the increasing deafness which even she herself could not understand (a curse on her father), poorly armed as a child — did she for the rest of her life have to take up the weapons of a child against life? How could she do battle with the god of nature, armed only with the wooden sword of her childhood?

I can recall the first day the Germanic girl looked at me as a man, Miss X. I had just returned from Europe and she had made even greater progress as the ingénue of the beach; the cunning connoisseur of the commercial traveler's own cunning in hotels; the initiate to sex experiences with fiery but inept rugby players in cars that are meant for transport and not love. My self-confidence was fresh, my clothes were of European cut, Miss X, to the delight of my consumption-racked aunt who had provided me generously with money, my sojourn in the unknown took place at a time when it carried a certain allure and romance. I was the young man who had been exposed to the whole world across the sea and who returned, estranged in the eyes of the guardians of national identity, an object of envy to the ones who stayed home, something of a deserter to the dear old matrons, a cognoscente in the eyes of the girls whose scorching imaginations pictured him sleeping with all of Zola's Nanas.

She was wearing the wrong clothes, my spring bride, that first evening in the home of my consumption-racked aunt: expensive, but too chintzy, with a heavy brunette perfume that clashed violently with the simplicity of the sunburned, athletic blond heroine of beach and salt water. Oh, she was impressed by the intoxicated charm of my aunt, the lazy, costly simplicity, the adventure of a different kind of civilization that she would later come to hate with an unutterably bitter rancor.

The manic-depressive stage comes later, Miss X, to all who are cursed with a false notion of elevated suffering. It came at a stage when she could avenge herself with the fact that her misjudged butcher-father had left her more than the rest; it came when her ten years of being desirable (when she could triumph over my aunt) were abruptly brought to an end in a Karmann Ghia behind a Karoobush; it came when my consumption-racked aunt had also to endure the humiliation of death; it came when she could compare, swinging back and forth on her crutches, leisurely in her noiseless world, the effete product of the hated, emasculated world of writing with her own short-lived triumph, when she was the goddess of battle in a young, alive land, when she could forget even her barrenness and use it as an asset in the rage of living that flooded the entire world after the war. She lost her undying youth, Miss X, in a world that promises undying youth to all attractive women. The god of nature used her, abused her, and left her with crutches and deafness because she could not comprehend. He destroys the uninformed, Miss X; he tortures the informed, but that's a different kind of suffering and you must take care, Miss X. That's my fear for you, my 18-year-old nymph. There can only be a choice of one for you, Miss X.

"That disturbs me, Mr. Y. But things like that don't happen in my world!"

"Forgive me my insensitivity, Mr. Y. I am 18 and I don't have your awareness of death and your guilt."

57

"But I am jealous, Mr. Y, of Laura; and I am restless because she disturbs me. Who is Laura? Do you often speak to her? Laura is very close to me; it is as though she is a man, as though she has the selfish little breasts of a man. She disturbs me, Mr. Y, and I want to warn you, but I don't know against what."

I told my Russian everything in the sunny park, but everything melted away into the sun and into my Russian's eyes that had known greater suffering. She had had her share in a world that is indescribable to us. She sees only the passing years and she unashamedly admires the gifts of the gods in herself: the balance that lets her triumph over the nymph and the 44-year-old woman who is a child. She has a mature sense of purpose and she offers her ripe fruits of love to the hack, who, as a writer, lives in too many worlds at once and, as a result of the dissemination, stands in danger of losing everything in all those worlds.

"But who is Laura?" my Russian asked with a patient smile, her hand in mine, on our walk through the patches of light and shade in the park.

Who was Laura? I looked back over the years, to Angélique, to Princess Ira von Liebenstein, and to the unformed, elusive inconnue in all my books.

She picked kukumakrankas with me in the dune fields, my dear Russian; she was the girl on the horse beside the sea. Our lives were beyond the sight of the outside world; there was love and death around every corner; we slept on haystacks beneath stars and in moonlight, wrapped in each other's arms under the very eyes of our trusting parents. Laura and I knew each other and came to know each other in the Biblical sense with a wonderful innocence. The spring scent of Laura; the flight of Laura among proteas on the white sand; the body of Laura in the swimming pool, weaving against mine, and the dark red nipples as the shoulder straps slid down, sinking down into the water, and the quivering contact as we held our breath to bursting point; Laura in the bathroom through the green window, my green nymph covered with sunlight soap; Laura with her thigh against mine under the table; Laura halfheartedly warding off my seeking hands while we played rummy; Laura on whom I spent all my energy and my teen-age years in dreams and in so many ways. Laura of the warm lounge and misty rain outside; Laura of the Christmas tree; Laura of the children's parties; Laura of hearths and burning logs; Laura when the wind whistled through the blue gums; Laura of the white cloud floating through an ink-blue sky; Laura of ghosts and terror; Laura of treasure hunts and secret passages; Laura of the woodpile and the keen-edged ax cutting through the wood knots; Laura of pigeons and chickens and rabbits; Laura of comics, sweet sweat and fresh bread; Laura of gangs and coal sheds; Laura of ice cream and tepid sea water; Laura of feather beds and telephone wires buzzing in the night; Laura of homework and punishment; Laura of radio-phonographs and serials; Laura of dolls and toy motorcars; Laura of tea sets and colored pieces of cloth; Laura suddenly strange and incomprehensible; Laura suddenly gone — and who was Laura? What did she look like?

Something in me goes ice-cold and I can't breathe. Laura has crumbled to ashes. My aesthetic uncle was dead, my consumption-racked aunt and I were completely alone. I carry the ashes of Laura with me in my adulthood and I know one failure after another. I babble incantations, I dream dreams, but all that comes out of the shallow subconscious and not from the vast unconscious where Laura is buried. I plunge myself into a dangerous sea, yet I bob along on the surface; I seek Laura everywhere — but Laura is hermetically sealed and all the heat and all the repetitions cannot make her reappear. I burn my freckle-faced bride in the smelting furnace, we burn together for three days, but nothing happens. There were three of us; the orphan, the consumption-racked widow and Laura-Luna, the moon. Now we are three again — a duplication of the mystery that will repeat itself again and again until the transformation takes place — I, with my Hermes typewriter, my Russian, and the pale, white X. Shall we three seek the *ecclesia spiritualis* together? We three in this world where the Logos rules? Will the world understand our longing for the unknown Anthropos?

The hack has to play the role of mediator, the great peacemaker, the hot-aired ape of God. Can you imagine him, in his white cottage, right next to the sea, built by his friend the homosexual architect, the spiritual hermaphrodite, as the little flame burns feebly?

Miss X, you told of your dream; here is mine.

I am taking leave of someone next to a shiny train that is to travel from west to east. I feel sad and terror stricken. Then I move all along the line westward and come to a high, concrete construction. With difficulty I climb right to the top, and there I see, reaching into infinity, a lake or catchment dam. It is not full, because I can make out islands as well as the original four streams or rivers that feed it. It comes as a shock because I did not expect anything like it. And I am disappointed because the dam or lake is not full.

The Many Forms of Fear

I FEEL THE ICE-COLD HAND of fear around my heart. Fear of what? Can it be fear of the Cossack, over the shoulder of my beloved; of his elegant bullies in their white shirts flanking him; fear of his circus pageant? How can there be fear in a place where children play leapfrog, and where an old man eats fish and chips, a newspaper spread open across his knees, the week-old news fresh through the oil stains? I know the Cossack's eyes well; I can picture them in my imagination: the vulnerable, soft eyes of someone who is compelled by love and tradition to take vengeance. There he comes, the Chmielnicki of the sunny park. And I am the Sabbethai Zebi who enthralls the apocalyptic fantasy of twentieth-century women and who incites them to give utterance to their deepest primordial desires. How lost the Cossack and I are in our respective roles, how incapable of coping with life! The Cossack is powerless before the fusion of the erotic and the mystic, the demonic root of love. He threatens us deliberately with his thickset henchmen, paper ghosts of his own past. He is without weapons, the Don Cossack, a wide-eyed warrior against the spiritual magician, his heretic wife in the arms of a hack, a prey to Shabbethainism and to her own orgiastic desires. The moment of truth is approaching, alike for the helpless persecutor and the helpless persecuted, the accursed false Messiah, in a Victorian park, bequeathed from a sunny time by a sunny aunt for a delicate game with life.

We would all rather have gone dancing together at the Cellars or in the grottoes of the city than to have gathered here: on the Tivoli stage out of the days of a consumption-racked woman, who has guilelessly also bequeathed a battlefield for the old and the new. The Cossack, over the shoulder of my beloved, and I, in her arms, have no choice because everything is lost in this park, Perte Sèche, which is incidentally also the name of the farm of my Hasidic uncle who used to dance when everyone else was working.

Fear is of course indescribable, Miss X, when one cannot describe the object of one's fear. And I fear for all of us, but I cannot tell why. It hangs like an ice stalactite in the air; something snaps and a bone-white sword pierces your brain, down, down into your heart. And then there is nothing left; nothing to give any clue to the deadly instrument that wipes out all trace of itself.

There was fear in my terror-ridden dream when the train was about to start moving from west to east; there was fear when my aunt and I looked at the cornflower in the magical wheat fields while my uncle was harvesting; there was fear when I could not find my Valkyrie among the colored lights; and there is the indefinite fear that comes over me as I sit here writing to you now. Yet my uncle lost his life years later, away from his wheat fields in his working yard; my Valkyrie, her soul many parties after the first red-lantern evening; you yourself, your urge to live, far away in the future removed from my prophecy, possibly the victim of the human condition when you have long forgotten me; and my consumption-racked aunt, without imaginable sense or reason, unexpectedly one day, her desire for sunny life. My fear is centered in the approaching movement of the dream train, Miss X. The carriages are shiny and new; the smoke from the locomotive clouds dark in the sky — black clouds of departure.

I was standing at my aunt's grave with the Valkyrie by my side, the eyes of the men fixed on her. The heavens were steely gray and rainy, as though my uncle were also present with the whimsicality of his own departure; the speeches and prayers were done; the few wreaths were scarcely sufficient to cover the little brown heap of earth; the seventeen people who attended the funeral looked somber in their coats — and I looked at the meager gathering and I wondered whether seventeen people were all that my aunt could have collected during her colorful life, because when one subtracts the doctor, the preacher, the lawyer and the night sister (who admired her because she died so quietly), and not counting the officials and the undertaker, so few are left. Icy fear curdled my heart: was this the fate of a vivacious individual? She gave me a part of her life as big as a world because my aunt was the seed of the twenties when everything was still an undifferentiated beginning; she was the elegant inspiration of my teenhood which she inaugurated with a laugh; she was the tease who saved my early adulthood from pompousness; she was, at her last, the one who, in a nascent tragedy, could acknowledge its wryly comical aspect with acceptance, and who made me able to cast out bitterness. She was also cruel, my aunt, because she was part of a civilization that could participate cynically in the death throes of its own dying ritual.

I looked, in those last moments of sacred stillness, at the fraudulence of those present: the tired physician, his beard blue and his eyes weak with weariness of the everlasting funerals that are part and parcel of his lucrative but time-consuming profession; the preacher, who, like his colleague in the flesh, has impersonalized death for his own peace of mind; the night sister, who had seen my aunt die quietly and was a connoisseur of birth and death; my Valkyrie, charming in black, not quite indifferent under the eyes of men; the high priest of the interment, in his top hat, proud of the mechanized apparatus that made my aunt's coffin disappear into the earth so noiselessly, becomingly, perfectly; the Coloured gravediggers who leapt with thuds onto her coffin and finished off their day's work with a song in their hearts; Piet Paling, the half-mad dracula of every funeral, which he attends in his threadbare suit; and the little cluster of strangers shaking hands and murmuring comforting Biblical texts, the Everymen of life and death. And I also looked at myself, somewhat dazed, a little lost in the social situation, and totally lost in a wider context. Indeed there was fear in the handful of earth that slapped onto my aunt's coffin.

When my Valkyrie wife, finely splintered, lay in hospital, I was lightly filled with fear by all the passageways, and all the somber lifts conveying food, cadavers or patients indiscriminately. Had it not been for the injured owner of the Karmann Ghia, the pleasant seducer and cause of my wife's misery, I should have visited that lodging house of infirmity far less often. He was pleasant company, the cricket player, in his penance (he reminded me a trifle of my aunt) and he made the countless visits a good deal easier for me. It was good to see how the broken Valkyrie made light of her agony when she saw us together before her bed. (In contrast with the times when, alone and awkward, I had to witness how wordlessly, staring wildly in her misery, she cursed her pain in which I was implicated.) I made certain that we appeared together, and that contributed a great deal to the recovery of the broken Valkyrie. (I cannot be grateful enough to the cricket player for his contribution.) It was a fascinating triangle, those visits of ours: a triumph of civilization. And it was good to see my Valkyrie fighting: clean, delightfully perfumed, her eyes shining bravely, still and calm and pretty in her bed (lipstick dark on her pale face, the mascara a black contrast; the interesting bewilderment which filled me with love and admiration). How we enjoyed those joint visits! There was a bond between me and the cricket hero. It was six months of a peculiar sort of life, and later we three, like old campaigners, often recalled those days with understandable sentimentality.

Ice-cold fear? That came in between — those shocking days, whenever I was alone, and when I saw my broken Valkyrie's eyes cloud over when no one else appeared in the doorway with me.

Fear, Miss X? Ask my beloved Russian. She knows a different kind of fear from yours and mine. She laughs at our subtleties. Have you ever heard the stutter of small arms in the night and the drone of bombers en route to their unknown destination? And the clanking of tanks on fields of ice and soldiers in pitch darkness suddenly visible in the light of shells? You can listen to the radio's "Victory Review," but it would mean very little indeed to you.

Miss X, Miss X, I am sorry. Your own fear has the same validity as hers. I should not disparage you. Not by holding you up against the Russian, because you both live in the same world today, and you are both subject to the same toll of our time. A mean or a heroic past are equally bloody unimportant. Fear is a fear is a fear is a fear.

Fear! Pheasants flying through the air. My aesthetic uncle lifted his shotgun, he swung it over the dunes, over the hills, over Berg River, over corn-gold, and brought down delicious dishes for us (his household: himself, my aunt and me). Our family numbered billions like the sand on the shore. (But my aunt had precisely seventeen at her funeral. On behalf of the family, our sincere thanks to them.) His double-barreled shotgun thundered against the clouds, and pheasants rained down trailing wings upon proteas and white sand. I was standing on a dune, and I saw the dead bird arching through the sky, and the prickles of my fear of the unknown spread and scattered against the arch of its death like the bird shot from my uncle's powerful gun.

Fear is the pitch-black locomotive about to move from west to east: the iron beast coming through the fog, mighty with the roar of its prehistoric might. The departure is a holy drama and the platform is strewn with precious relics and magical instruments; and the shiny carriages are filled with faceless passengers. (Do I hear the voice of Laura? Do I see her face for a split second among all the faceless ones?) Kundry struggled to find her voice and she keened into the gloomy night: the sleep of death that will not come to deliver her. The S.A.R. locomotive whistles in the dark, the reprobate Knight of the Holy Grail from the years of our childhood that has become the monster of our middle age. The consumption-racked woman is transformed in the violent departure: she gleans enough youth and beauty again to seduce the young man, alone on the platform of lost stations. The train leaves and thunders against the Swartland mountains. The young fool, the butterfly of his uncle's wheat fields, who has grown wise through compassion, gives a chaste kiss to the transformed Laura who disappears, doomed, in rags. She dies as the train leaves and in the light of the moon, imbued with heavenly beauty, a dead pheasant, with widespread wings, glimmering in the white radiance, drifts down gently upon the youthful guard.

The platform disappears, the station crumbles with the years, but the *clang-clang-clang* of the bells on the locomotive is still echoing against the mountains. There is fear in the heart of the middle-aged protector of the sacraments, because after the death of the witch-nymph, the monster locomotive, S.A.R., still *clang-clang*s his warning unceasingly with prehistoric might of steam and fire against the invisible electricity of future locos.

Amfortas (Pty.) Ltd. and Gurnemanz (Publishing Co.) gave the hack an advance on his next best seller, which allowed him to build his white house next to the sea. It's a stark house of clean, snow-white painted bricks against a blue sea: a skeleton of our time.

Fear, Miss X, fear for the fate of the child of the widow who could reconcile conflicting elements in herself — the consumption-racked old woman, the black woman of life and death, the *meretrix* of the forties, when she could offer love at cost price, the woman without husband, but the mother of all the young soldiers en route to the front, my fleeting counterpart, the sweetly cruel *vitua*, the moon, the virgin at the center of the earth, *praegnans* in a next dream, mother of the *filius philosophorum* (the hack, but "that's not what I meant, Y, Y . . ."), the bountiful earth in which corn grows with black rust and dew on the ears, the black widow spider, who bites, as dangerous as an adder, she-devil, Holy Virgin, alchemistic mother, *prima materia*, elixir of life *in potentia*, the lake of my dreams . . .

But the lake is only half-full, half-full in my dreams, and fear clutches at me: is there enough, is there enough of the secret liquid nucleus to repair the disintegration, to reconstruct Osiris after the death of Gabritius?

Fear, Miss X, for the hack in the gruesome drama of man trapped in his psychic destiny, the endless striving after unity with thousands of wrecks along the way, where incest, cruelty, false mother love, murder, hatred, castration and all forms of tyrannical love form part of the crucible from which rebirth must flow like the fertile gold of my uncle's wheat fields.

Fear, Miss X, for you, Venus, Luna, nymph and the eternal young woman, and for myself, the winged Mercury, the reconciler. How shall I ever be able to bring the opposites together? You, my nymph, my manic-depressive wife, my consumption-racked aunt and my lonely Russian. I feel like Yesod, Miss X. All of you are Malchuth in four forms. I shall go in unto you; I shall make water flow in you through fifty sluices; Shekinah will be present; you will become gardens and especially you, my nymph, will be fruitful according to your deepest desires. The man shall be above, and the woman below like in the cabalistic dream.

But I am afraid, Miss X . . . There are four streams in the lake of my dream, and in my dream the lake is not full because I can see the four streams: four slender streams through the mists. Perhaps I am simply paranymph, and I am afraid, Miss X, for all of you and for myself.

Fear, Miss X, that stretches across all the years that formed me: fear in the evening as a child alone in my aunt's house, fear for the mystery of the years to come. Fear when the world I know lies in pieces the next morning. Fear when in my wandering I try to regain my source, and all that is left are vague, faintly outlined memories that swell like lazy waves against styliform incidents, the rocks of breakwaters and the pillars of piers as we all bop under colored lights on the promenades.

Fear, Miss X, when I looked into my aunt's eyes after she had asked me: "Are you happy, Y, Y?" And I see her face before mine: the vulnerable face that she turned squarely to mine so that I had to look at her — the eyes that had suddenly gone grim with an unknown suffering in spite of the lost little devils that flickered forth determinedly; the straight nose over which her skin anxiously pulled into a thousand little wrinkles; the lips creased and peeling with the remains of crimson putty; the flesh on her cheeks pressed paper-thin by a taut skin over the skull that would be turned to heaven six feet underground within a year or two; the glow of her thin blood crossing her face in a network of tiny arteries; the skeleton enfolded in flowered silk — the remnants in rags of a dynamic spirit that used the body like a vampire and which surely, after her imminent death, would wander in search of a temple that could bear the intensity of that spiritual conflict. The spring tides of life and death in her: the paradox that is a divine gift; the pianissimo and the fortissimo; the depths and the heights of the comic opera in which the mundane and the godly in their battle against each other reach a thundering climax.

Are you someone like Madame Blavatsky, my aunt; are you the greatest charlatan of all times, or is your consumption-racked body really the cosmic fount of rebirth?

How shall I know, the hack, here in front of the pendulum, my wife, who swings and swings against the blue sea that swells and swells in front of my snow-white cottage designed by my friend the homosexual architect?

Illusion or reality?

I see us all together: in that moment when everyone was alive, on the dunes and among the heather, with birds in flight while the hunters made the heavens glitter with buckshot; when the buckshot dropped the roebuck next to a protea; my spring bride the fleeting hind on white sand where puff adders strike; my butcher-father in the mystique of blood and incest; my aesthetic uncle trapped, knotted and tortured in the mechanism of his steel spider; my ice-bound Russian with a longing for warmth that would melt the ice, in the arms of her misplaced generator, the hack.

I see the anxious eyes of the enigmatic Madame Blavatsky in you all, her total commitment; I see her face like that of my consumption-racked aunt, a medium and a sorceress, seeking Koot Hoomi who lives in Tibet. The searching eyes, the hollows in the cheeks, the paleness of longing for truth.

Madame Blavatsky grew fat and often refused to die;

but everyone talks of her eyes. I see the four eyes of four women shock-still in the suspended animation of total search.

I am utterly alone, Miss X; I look into your four pairs of eyes and life is too much for me.

Who Are You, Miss X, and Who Are We?

YOUR LETTERS ARRIVE once a fortnight and I wait anxiously for the mail to be sorted. There is a lyrical quality in your letters: I see the fine, large letters that look like printing; your total contempt for any form of punctuation; the easy flow of your thoughts; the challenging baring of yourself. I try to build up an image of you from what you write, because you are no more than a name, as I read your letters among my manuscripts and the ever-changing sea before me reflects your own mood of three days ago, and while my manic-depressive, crippled wife directs her host of servants in the preparation of demoniac meat dishes in the milk-white, neon-lit American kitchen.

"I always wait for evening before I write," you write. "Now evening falls bluer and bluer upon my beloved . . . and my eyes grow blacker and blacker and by midnight I shall stand in front of the mirror and try to look deeper into my eyes with a sense of wonder. Not in the whole . . . is there a girl with such deep, black eyes at twelve o'clock at night."

"When I get up in the morning my eyes are nothing, they simply reflect the light on the bathroom wall and the ice-white windows."

What do you look like, Miss X?

"I know what kind of women you like, Mr. Y. Dark. Slightly rounded features. Black hair, dark eyes and plum mouth as ripe as plums."

She nervously draws a key ("to my heart, Mr. Y") and a little bottle of antihistamine, Picasso-like, fine as the threads in a female spider's web.

Using the watercolor paint box of my childhood, she draws a green streak across the page, the green of the window through which I saw Laura dancing in sunlight soap on the wet bathroom floor.

"You like green women, Mr. Y. You like smallish women, women with pretty noses: smallish and very straight. Large mouths, fairly wild eyes far apart with untidy lashes. Golden hairs on the back that grow right down to the coccyx. Impatient, restless hands and contemptuous shoulder blades, a manageable bosom not too big, smallish apple buttocks. Forehead smelling of honey, women with warm, white feet and white, short nails, veins that stand out slightly on the hands and square teeth — straight."

I thought of you, Miss X, when my Russian questioned me about you and I answered evasively in the sunny park. Will you forgive me if for the moment I write you off as invisible for the sake of peace? I am in the heart of a sunny day, in a park, at the heart of a noisy city, and all around me there is movement: a corpse on its way to the morgue, a beggar on the make, Madame Gorgon intoxicated with pity, coffee and tea in the gardens, hoses watering cannas, children enjoying the freedom of the park like pet animals, robbers innocent in the uniforms of milkmen — smelled out by Alsatians who can feel the tingling and challenge of evil in their nostrils.

There is stillness in this moment around which my whole life whirls like a merry-go-round.

There is the stillness of great meaning: moments of

stillness, not for vast decisions, but important for the adventures of an ordinary person — should you turn left or right, should you put your weakness at stake and risk eating a peach, should you betray your great-grandfather, should you sacrifice your peaceful existence for the transient ecstasy of an exhilarating transgression? Or should you, hack, be strong and selfish enough to still the trumpeting of your manic-depressive wife, to wipe out the memory of your consumption-racked aunt, to let the butcher-father choke in the blood of his house, to let your nymph-in-letters smother in the swamp of her teen despairs and be just toward the Russian who is really, at this moment, asking you the only question that has any immediate meaning?

We are both 44 and that's not an age where you have time to gape romantically at life. I look into the eyes of my Russian and at the Cossack closing in and I suddenly realize how little time is left to reconcile all of you, because I need all four of you, and all four of you are part of me, or something in me will disintegrate and I shall become more than one.

It is in fact a vital decision, Miss X. I must be able to identify all of you; I must be able to reconcile those conflicting elements in myself — for my own sake and for you all. My consumption-racked aunt, my manic-depressive wife and my fiery Russian were a symbolic triad of growth; and now there is you, Miss X, and in the fourfold aspect of our union lies true totality, the peace and repose for the future. But you are the invisible, Miss X. You are the unknown planet in the Heimarmene that is about to destroy me, unless with my Hermes-Ambassador typewriter I can find the golden mean.

What do you look like, Miss X? I have to rely on the description of women you project on me. What are you trying to say? I feel like taking you by the shoulders and shaking you while I look into your invisible face and ask that question again and again of you and of myself.

She drew her hand and four clowns leaping into the air. She also drew me a "sea gooseberry with people in it," and the sea gooseberry is a man and a woman encircled by the coils of a sea snake.

I got into my car and drove to the address given in her letters; I made ninety-degree left and right turns through the symmetrical postwar suburb on my way to the street and the number of her house. Suddenly I slowed down, like someone afraid, in the midst of the neat uniformity of middle-class prosperity, and I stopped in front of a house. I recognized the house by her letters: the slate roof, the fine lawn, the swimming pool in the back yard and the shrubs in the well-cared-for garden. Beneath a liver-red wild plum I saw a girl on a chaise longue, her legs wrapped in iron calipers: a beautiful blond mermaid in her armor. We looked at each other, I over the steering wheel, she over the book she had been reading, while a light wind ruffled the leaves of the tree softly. Then she suddenly held the book before her eyes and I could see her moving her head anxiously from side to side. I could have died of indecision and then I drove on quickly, down the street to the next corner, where I stopped again and looked around blindly to find my bearings. And then I saw the name of the street, in yellow, on the sign post, and it was a strange name and I had been quite wrong.

Back, at full speed, to Princess Ira von Liebenstein (Laura) where reassuringly she still haunted the large estate on the mountainside. The sea was rough and mighty waves thundered against the beach. My crippled, manic-depressive wife welcomed me reassuringly with her reproaches, on a higher frequency in the trumpeting, as though she were still in telepathic communication with me and could penetrate my most secret motives on the trite plane of her own outlook on life. Hysterically she rocked back and forth on her crutches and I was at once filled with tenderness: how can it be just for the ice gods to return heroically from the battlefield with noble scars while the snow queen is not allowed a single scar? I decided at once to write her a series of letters, under the name of the missing cricket hero. I was already composing them in my mind while she stormed in the distance: romantic letters, lovingly addressed to my crippled Valkyrie.

"I wanted to visit you this afternoon, Miss X, just to see what you look like and who you are, but at the last moment I decided not to do so, because I found myself in the wrong street and that was a warning. It is better that we never see each other, Miss X."

"That would probably be best, Mr. Y. I admire your courage, your purposefulness and your maturity — and your judgment, care and discretion, Mr. Y."

"Don't be ironic, Miss X."

My manic-depressive, crippled, deaf Valkyrie wife received her first letter and rocked blushingly, rhythmically backward and forward on her crutches. She was noticeably friendlier toward me and read me imaginary sentences from the letter of a distant, forgotten cousin. A

calm came over her and she lied to me with the same innocence as during the years when her wordless lies drove me
to frenzy. Every day she devoted more care to herself:
her hair was regularly shampooed and done, with interesting streaks among the flaxen gold (her hair had remained
unscathed). The coarseness of her face, a legacy from her
butcher-father, the product of self-pity and the ravages of
time, was carefully, slowly hardened into a beauty mask
that she built attentively and deliberately with the most
expensive cosmetic preparations.

The softness in her empty blue eyes when she received
the letters from the cricket hero spurred me to write her
ever-better ones. I wrote letters that I could not write to
my invisible Miss X — to her alone. The letters to my invisible X drew level on another plane. The one woman
was assimilated into the other and became identified with
her — a triumph for the creative power of the artist; an
artistic faculty of creative energy to experience undifferentiated content in presymbolic form and then to project
it. I was rapidly bringing about a reconciliation while my
Valkyrie wife repaired the upper half of her body, and
while my nymph blossomed in the unexpected warmth of
her newly fired father-lover.

Months of reconciliation and unfoldment while even the
hardness of my Valkyrie's cosmetic mask, under an inner
glow, began to lose its hardness and softly began to radiate an inner beauty — while my unknown X began to take
form: a playful, deeply feeling, teasing nymph, now intro-
duced for the first time to the first stage of her longed-for
initiation. Months of middle-aged ecstasy while my Valkyrie sent her letters to every address I could possibly

imagine; letters which would disappear into the files of the postal service to return, possibly after twenty years, from the past, stamped address unknown, in red. (It gives me a certain sense of satisfaction: the endless detective hunt of the postal service; their contribution to the fate of a single missing person — the Mounties of our childhood who always get their man.) Months of nascence in which my invisible X, without being able to lay her teen finger on one single sentence, could yet sense a surrender in both of us; months in which she could find a spiritual fulfillment; months in which she could see herself as the companion of Amor: the *stirb und werde* for which she longed so passionately.

It was, honestly, a triumph of projection which lies at the roots of creativity.

Life became more pleasant: my snow-white cottage on the flank of the mountain above the sea, built by my homosexual friend the architect, became a miniature pleasure garden of spiritual harmony. When the telephone rang, it was my Valkyrie who, skidding across the smooth floor in her haste, was the first to lift the receiver in vain; when the post was delivered, she watched with anxious eyes as I won the impossible ground with youthful bounds and, with accounts and newspapers, produced two magical letters: one for her and one for me, letters that we handled like treasures as we smiled at each other and each could be seen in his little corner, devouring the contents of the pages with greedy eyes. And afterward we were soft and friendly toward each other; we would even drink a bottle of wine with our dinner; we would chat by candlelight at table with a civilized indulgence on the new level of peaceful coexistence that we had recovered unexpectedly. She would ask how my writing was progressing (I have little opportunity to write: the piles of letters take up all my time); I would courteously inquire after all her countless boring friends. And later . . . when we both, genial after the wine, took up our pens, we would write until late into the night, letters fifteen pages long for the will-o'-the-wisp on the ocean, right in front of our snow-white cottage, reflecting glistening water.

Yet I feel unsure, Miss X, toward the other two of the foursome that is now the center of my life: my Russian, here and now, and the ghost of my consumption-racked aunt out of the past who is rapidly becoming less and less real for all who knew her, except for me. Great truths are concealed in the archetypes of one's childhood, Miss X.

My consumption-racked aunt and I still wander through the park where the conductor radiated his magic upon her; she addresses the wisdom of those years to me in aphorisms; I myself become captive to her time; she becomes a well from which I shall draw for the rest of my life. (Perhaps you, Miss X, will someday be just as bound to the founts of your teen youth, of which I and my letters are possibly also a part.)

A motorboat on the Bree River was on the point of departure. Stella with the dimples in her cheeks, the green-eyed seductress of all the men in their thirties, the dangerous flapper menaced my uncle with a life urge equal to her own, there where everyone gathered to travel through the mouth to the deep sea with flags flying on my uncle's powerful motorboat. My consumption-racked aunt moved with the stream, a long cigarette holder in her hand, two young men at her feet, two secretary birds from the Swartland, leaders of the dance and progressive farmers, exuberant sowers of wild oats — wild males on their fiery way to restful destinations with women from good families, chairmen of future farmers' unions, cornerstones of the church, later bidders for the farm of my uncle who died on the battlefield of agricultural industry, a sacrifice to the rural implements of war, the mechanical monsters that sacredly harvest wheat and sacredly harvest the lives of men.

The motorboat droned in the water, wailed hysterically over the waves, and conveyed my aesthetic uncle's jubilant guests to the open sea and his own downfall.

(Miss X, Miss X, can I ever make you comprehend something in my world which is also true in your world? And I know you will ask the same question someday of some unknown Y in the future. Someone like you are at this moment. And you will try in vain to explain to him the mystery of your teen years.)

The motorboat thundered, like the locomotive, out to the open sea. The deck was full of boisterous passengers and everywhere there were ribbons and trumpets while we children on the shore saw something, something more disappearing behind the waves left by my uncle's massive boat.

My butcher-father was one of the passengers: his Stetson squarely on his head, his liverish face twisted into a multivalent grin about the approaching downfall of my gay uncle, his Valkyrie safely surrounded by cute young men from the Swartland, his unknown son-in-law's eyes shining in ecstasy for the powerful departure, with the song of Laura conjured up in his heart by the screws that flung sea-river water up into the skies.

Did *anyone* know, on the pleasure boat and on the shore, how one and all, many years later, in terms of the rational, hard reality of the future, would try to reconcile the past with the present in the same kind of boat at the same river mouth at the same beach that is now strewn with thousands of holiday makers? In a certain sense, that boat never returned and it sails still with its merry passengers, with the tinsels and trumpets of their time, on the Indian Ocean, the prenatal depthless sea, like the *Flying Dutchman* with its captain, my uncle, who, after his death, still shows his face to fishermen in False Bay, to the Prince of Wales, and to everyone along the southern coast of Africa: the accursed on his endless voyage, our only Voortrekker on water in search of the tantalizing truth that still eludes us all — my impractical uncle with his monster boat of the deep sea. How we children cried, we children on the shore, as the boat disappeared! Even my *Walkürchen,* for her Teutonic father, his face liver-red under the Stetson, away from his butcheries and the orderliness of his carcasses awaiting him in perfect symmetry precise as he disappeared with the others into the licentiousness of salty spray.

Poor little freckle faces, poor burbling sucklings of the twenties and thirties that wander in parks today and give themselves hell because of their fear. Because nobody really returned from that sea voyage.

Miss X, Miss X. Could I be Ahasuerus who ranges abroad in loneliness while everyone around him, all his loved ones, endure the same agony endlessly? Am I taxed with the curse of knowledge, the cold eye in the middle of my forehead slowly opening to see the terrible truth?

Tonight I talked to a teen-ager — a substitute for you, Miss X — and she told me (her eyes grass-green beneath the arc of her hair, her little waist supple under the mini) of her thirteen-year-old cousin who does ballet on Mondays, and Tuesdays belles-lettres, and Wednesdays karate, and Thursdays diving, and Fridays singing, and Saturdays sex and Sundays Sunday school with a pale white eunuch.

Where do you fit in, Miss X? What do you look like, Miss X — as at this moment I wrestle with the love of my Russian and the ghost of my aunt?

I weigh my aunt (44 when she died) and my Russian (44 in my arms) on the scale of the meretrix, the statue of Justice in front of the Supreme Court. Two women of 44 in the timeless scale. Two worlds and two women, of different times but bound to the same period as child and woman, who achieved a balance in the severe, blind objectivity of the graven image.

"I can remember nothing," said my Russian. "I can remember nothing." And I could feel her hand go rigid and wet in mine. And it seemed the park grew cold that sunny day, while my grim and remote Russian tried to push away her whole past and then finally said: "We gathered blackberries in the woods. That's all I can remember. All those blackberries in the woods."

I held her lovingly in my arms to bridge that abyss between us. Will we ever be able to find a meeting ground in that strange world of which I know nothing? She is like my consumption-racked aunt who is trying to give me something out of her own phantom world; but she does not succeed except for glimpses that fall on me like rays of light and that fill me with a plaintive sadness and yearning for something I long for but that I cannot express in words: an urgent truth in that radiation and an obscure, formless understanding on my part because I am a writer, who, even in weakness, can sense truth in its undifferentiated form — a presymbolic insight that later, once the symbol is there, allows me to comprehend the range of the symbol.

We pour light upon each other, each from his own strange world, and we find each other lonely in these beams of light casting back and forth on each other, with a feeling of affinity, as the source of life within ourselves generates the streams of light.

"I remember my uncle," the Russian said suddenly, and her eyes glistened with the play of memory and imagination. "Uncle . . . and he played the violin at four in the morning." Now her eyes glittered under the kohl. "Every morning he collected ice stalactites and arranged them on a table: a whole village, with houses and people, and sometimes it melted away and sometimes it was so cold that his village stayed frozen on the table. He had the very best bed of cabbages and he never picked them. He drew lines with his rake between the rows of vegetables; black lines in the black turf. I was four," she said. My elegant Russian, a little girl of four!

Dear Jesus, my aesthetic uncle, not only the skipper of the *Flying Dutchman,* not only the playboy on his motorboat (his boater awry in the wind), not only in the impractical mechanic of the Boland, but now also in distant far-off Russia!

I kissed my Russian lightly on her lips and she rejoiced in my understanding. I kissed her somewhat sadly because that's also not the whole truth. Her poor uncle . . . born in Russia or now, here?

Who are we, Miss X?

We are people in a dream, Miss X, where the mundane and the exoteric go hand in hand with the esoteric.

Last night I had a strange dream: I dreamed that I was sleeping in my room and that the floor was covered with water. I got up carefully because I knew I would slip and I should be cautious. I suddenly stumbled over a glass vase: a beautiful vase shining with all the colors of the rainbow. As I fell, I protected the vase: I enfolded it in the hollows of my arms and the glass remained intact.

Ma Tante

THERE IS SOMETHING of the gay nineties in her — "I wonder who's kissing her now . . . In the merry month of May . . . In the shade of the old apple tree, in the blossoms that you sent me, with a heart that is true . . . Hello, my lady! . . . Once you come home, my lady . . ."

And the *Lorelei, Ich weiss nicht was soll es bedeuten dass ich so traurich bin,* as my consumption-racked aunt sailed down the Rhine on Rhine wine, and she lifted her eyes to the romantic castles above the terraced vineyards. An orchestra played for her alone in a cellar in Innsbruck, and the ski instructor allowed her to give the violinist a bountiful tip. "In Vienna they drink white wine; here we drink red," he whispered in the ear of the slender virgin from the Boland. They waltzed the Prelude to the Act of Love, played by the thundering orchestra of merry Austrians. In an expensive place with purple lights, they were served estate wines at wooden tables by *mädchen* in checked aprons. She lost her virginity, but not her honor, in a hotel where everything was spotlessly fresh and from whose window she could see the rosy outline of an enormous snow peak in the distance the following morning. That was better than brackish furrows, and defloration became, to my aunt from the Boland, an initiation into the world of the *National Geographic* magazine, which

85

she collected by the hundreds in her refined room in her father's house in the Boland. Everything waltzed in the Boland and Swartland while she awaited her future mate who would come waltzing to her.

While unknown parents were giving birth to me, my aunt moved in the naughty twenties with my aesthetic uncle at her side: a dark-haired man with blue eyes, a pianist of unusual talent, a dreamer on haystacks, an Afrikaner with Spanish blood who could tread out flamenco rhythms for my aunt in their dance of love in Caledon, Heidelberg and Swellendam.

They moved together through the twenties: "Ring-ring the banjo, Hallelujah! How I love you, Swanee! Waiting for me, praying for me, down by the Swanee! Mammy! Mammy! The sun shines east . . . I'm a-comin' . . . The Robert E. Lee-e-e-e!" and a whistling and stamping and Black Bottom and the Charleston that my aunt could dance so well — her slender thighs exposed, snow-white flanks of love with tiny blue lines from varicose veins left by her only stillborn child.

The feeble thirties, the misleading feebleness of the thirties when everyone survived the depression and H. G. Wells's *Things to Come* was being filmed, and Schicklgruber announced the Prelude to the Act of War in beer halls before romantic Germanic gods which would be resurrected for the last time in an archetypal twilight, and while my Russian paid in fear and terror, while she was deflowered (the child with blackberries in her hands, and a vague memory of an uncle . . .) on a train, by Amor in armor, a panting primitive beast, a soldier of the state.

The roaring forties! The death of my uncle and the last years of the slender widow, the desolate Malchuth, my aunt, the holder of the pawn ticket to my writer soul.

Shall I be Yesod, *ma Tante*, will the Shekinah be present at the act of creation, shall I be able to restore the mystic union, the magical marriage, so you will say: that's what I meant, Y, Y. That's exactly what I meant . . . ?

I long incestuously for you, my aunt.

My Russian

My Russian, while her protector, the Cossack, closes in relentlessly, soon to put an end to forbidden love. A westernized Russian, out of touch with her past, caught up in a world of dead gods, the epitome of sterile Western refinement once she had rid herself of her youth.

She told me, for the first time, for our love's sake, and while the face of the Cossack loomed larger and larger over her shoulder.

There were fifty in the cattle truck on their way to a secret destination and the soldier with the white face took the girl in his arms to protect her against the cold while her parents stared with dazed, blind eyes into the unknown future, pathetic remnants of former proud merchant princes. The soldier crooned a children's song in her ear to reassure her: "Do you remember, little devushka . . . ?" And he also sang of his own past in his own village, tucked away in the snow. He told her of wolves and forests, and told her of half-forgotten legends from his childhood in the stinking train: of Stribog in the frost, Peroun in his fiery chariot, the oak fires that must

87

burn forever or you die, the stallion of Khors in the hunt, the warm blood surging through one's veins. He cuddled her more tightly to him and told her of the new world and the new order, because the memories were vague and his youth drew further and further from him. He told her about a future filled with wonder while his warm hands slipped under her blouse and petted the cold little breasts. He was soft and loving, the compassionate armored soldier, with the cigarette behind his ear. He slobbered babbling lullabies as he nibbled at her ear lobes; he folded her into his thick coat while he lifted her small dress and stroked her thighs. He pierced and broke the hymen unseen as the train shuddered on a curve and her scream was lost in the unbroken screech of the locomotive on the black rails through the pine woods. He pressed her tightly to him while he burbled toward her parents, and afterward, the sad animal, chatted reassuringly with them while he comforted their sobbing daughter and a flicker of life came into the blind eyes of the parents because of these few tokens of pity, among all the cruelty, from a soldier of the state. Her mother offered him a piece of their moldy bread, the little piece that was left over, and he accepted it, broke it in half and shared it with the weeping child that he cradled safely in his arms.

My lovely Russian, elegant, chic, in my arms of her own free will, and I looked into her eyes in which there was no fear and looked up into the vengeful eyes of the Cossack and I suddenly had the feeling that somebody was going to pay dearly for all the misery and all the bloody suffering.

My fiery Russian waiting for me, from the Boland and Swartland, to transform a distant violation into a violation of love in this sunny park, while her husband, the Cossack, Don Quixote with his Sancho Panzas, stormed his windmill. I moved and waved and swung as they closed in, with the passionate, weaving Russian, my beloved, in my arms.

The Valkyrie

Because she is deaf, she speaks like a computer endowed with the power of speech. There is a certain logic and a mechanical wisdom that I can't argue against. She has, like the Russian, her own past of suffering, and who am I, the hack, to compare the refinement of one kind of suffering with another? She booms from the chamber of her past; she is an electronic orchestra built into a six-foot body. Life dents her just as a car crash dents the fenders and the hood and the sides; but the battered body moves on, with a powerful engine and a shrill horn.

My Valkyrie wife's whole life consists of those years when she was whole and perfect; when she was at the peak of physical perfection; then she left me, understandably, groping in the shadows of the colored lights.

I need soft lights to enchant me . . .

She chimes like a bell on her crutches.

She feels ill at ease in the snow-white cottage built by my friend the homosexual architect. Everything is too white and too modern against the blue of the sea. There are too few colors: she looks for the red of her father's

Germanic butchery; the green of his counter; the purple of ox blood; the black covers of his ledgers.

She tolls as she swings on her crutches and calls out to something in the tolling of her carillon. But there is a flaw in the bell; and because everything is welded over to make it hang together, it sounds metallic and the cry is lost in the metal ring of her glockenspiel.

I see her when she was still my Brynhild-Brunhild-Laura; I see her behind the crutches and behind the shadows of her translucent light — far, far back when she came over the dunes of Witsand like a ribbok, a doe princess among the rest. My Valkyrie against the sea; among heather and proteas — against the mystery of that time. One day she fell and a thorn pierced her thigh: her snow-white thigh with the white thorn. The young Cape doctor cut it out — a young doctor fresh from the University of Cape Town, and he put his arm around her, cared for her and pampered her like the white soldier pampered my Russian. Did the doctor steal a march on the commercial travelers in his clinic? I like to think so. The medico in his worn blue blazer, that touch of snobbery that lifted him above us ordinary mortals. White sand, proteas, dunes and instant success! How could the nascent writer, with his incomprehensible words, compete with the incomprehensible actions of the practitioner? He married a girl from Dublin: black hair and blue eyes, and thank God she gives him hell. Did he sow the first germ in his seed? Are the rugby players, the cricket players, the spirits of her colored lights, the fruit of his clinical penis? Are the easy conquests of commercial travelers the aftermath of his selfish orgasm?

I think back further, to when she was pure Valkyrie.

When with the south wind in her hair and the salty tang of her teen-age body she was the *virgo intacta* of my imagination.

But all is saved, all is saved — thanks to the letters to her (exact copies of my letters to X) from the legendary cricket player with the winged pen of a writer. She rocks lightly backward and forward on her soft crutches. She dresses herself laboriously in dated Quant dresses. Above the mutilated parts she paints herself with paint brushes and adorns herself with all the preparations bought at their most expensive with the money of her godly butcher-father.

A six-foot woman on crutches, completely naked. First the panties with strips of lace, transparent except where a double layer of nylon is necessary for camouflage. Then a flesh-colored petticoat with embroidery which is a further interesting indication of the magic enchantment that exotic underwear holds for women in love, as though it were the true uniform in which their lovers could see them with x-ray eyes. Then a snow-white dress. It sinks over her, sticks, and scrapes tightly over her body to a mini length that she has calculated exactly for what is left of her figure. She sits on her stool in front of the mirror; the crutches are on either side of her; and in that position she is entirely whole. Perfumed, clean for her hero, the cricket hero, who bowls pure balls at the stumps she has prepared so diligently, along the wicket at which she worked for days and nights.

She paints her eyelashes with paint from India; she adds blue from Russia; she draws lines to the corners of her eyes with powder from China; she crimsons her lips with cochineal from desert cacti. She sprays herself lightly with an esoteric perfume from France for the hero of the letters.

She stands up, fits the crutches into the shaved hollows under her arms, and limps forward to meet her letters.

She rocks rhythmically backward and forward on her crutches and there is harmony in our house.

I read X's letters undisturbed and my desk is littered with the "manuscripts," documentary proof of betrayal. I also often think about what her butcher-father would have said over in his particular Valhalla, the Great Butchery beyond the clouds, among the etheric cadavers swaying to the beat of cosmic winds. I can imagine the old man, happy (because how can I complete a cameo of the Valkyrie without her thunder gods?') — happy in an eternity where he, wearing a blue apron, hairy arms laid bare, butcher knife in hand, slices cuts from heavenly carcasses while a colossal cash register rings up spiritual cents with a celestial ringing of bells. My happy butcher-father among the clouds, beside my consumption-racked aunt who waltzes with her shadow through a spacious heaven to the beat of a celesta; and beside my aesthetic uncle, the merry clown, whose feet juggle a heavenly globe while his mind is enmeshed in an astronomical map. Will he touch me on the shoulder three times with his butcher knife? I feel the bloody stroke of knighthood from my butcher-father as I stretch my talent to the utmost, while I compose letters and thereby demonstrate the value of literary art to high heaven. My butcher-father beams from the Great Butchery and a halo of pure white intestines settles around the head of one who has grown wise with pity.

He has heard the mystical voice; Amfortas on high with the wound in his side where his heart should be. My poor butcher-father. Who was his Kundry? Of which Laura was he aware in the darkness within himself? Did he not bleed when he bought the queens of the animal kingdom at twenty-five cents a pound and unveiled them on the abattoir block?

I see him, the generative fount of the Valkyrie, my snow goddess: the snow-white flower that grows dangerously out of frozen blood, the product of his icy spear that sowed poison.

How could he have known that the thundering sacrilege against the unknown mother (who was she?) of my Valkyrie would return in the emptiness that was his heart? I now understand the sterility and the sterilized air of his butcheries.

And what he did was that which is expected of a god. On his four-poster, one terrible night, above his butchery.

Is that not treachery from the omnipotent?

But, honestly, how could my Swartland butcher-father have been expected to realize the eternal meaning of betrayal?

Miss X

A cameo based on letters?

An 18-year-old, fiery as my Russian and sometimes heavy hearted, with a pen from which her thoughts flow freely, unrestrained, like the blood with which we occasionally stain the pages, and then everything congeals in broad daylight and I read her letters and say to myself: No! No! But the next instant I find nuances of comprehension advanced far beyond her years and part of the true life of conflicts and contradictions, the ambiguity and dichotomy of our earthly existence, but warm and tingling, down spirited and depressed, manic and depressive before the dim promise of the years that lie ahead (not so with my manic-depressive wife and me, who seek meanings in a 44-year wink of an eye).

A melancholy child who first projected her father on me ("I wish I were your child, Mr. Y!"); an unfolding young woman who becomes aware of her idealized animus-father in her lover; the child-woman weighed down by an image ("It's not a flesh-and-blood experienced reality, Mr. Y"). My dear nymph who changes quick as lightning, month after month, letter after letter, because her days and her months are the days and months of lightning change.

Miss X, a paper doll with writing on it.

All the flower petals, all the seeds, all the little hairs on her arm and the snippets from her dresses sent in a letter contrary to postal regulations, make her a character out of Jean-Claude van Itallie avant-garde theater: a tinfoil Lolita in the experimental theater of her teen existence.

A cameo of Miss X, 18 years?

I see her sometimes, like Laura, in passing. A girl in the grotesque mask of the sixties, with the curse of being forming a tiny wrinkle right in the middle of the wrinkled mark on her forehead where the third eye will open under the waterfall of her untamed hair. She is infinitely wiser than I. I cannot speak to her out of my own 18 years. She is the young adult, the mutation of our time; and she sends her barbs out twenty-six years ahead.

We feel both the sadness and the ecstasy. She rages against the treachery of God; I accept the treachery as part of the reality of life.

Only in our nonphysical letters can we bridge time. In the clichés of our letters the word becomes flesh.

A cameo of a nymph?

A cameo of Laura! A cameo of my Valkyrie when she was a silhouette against the blue sea! A cameo of my aunt in Innsbruck at the foot of a rosy mountain! A cameo of my Russian with blackberries in her arms in the black forest! That's asking too much of the imagination of a hack, *ma Tante*.

IT IS VERY NEARLY TIME for the park to close and it is as if
the Cossack were attuned to every emotion from every direction; as if with his calculation of time he had a primordial knowledge that everything in this archetypal park had
to come to an end at this particular stage; as if he, also,
conceived of the cosmic significance in the immediate per-
sonal relationships and situations. He and his two primeval beasts — two dark shadows, two gorillas with white
shirts glowing phosphorescently. It is time to close and it's
the end of security and of perfection and of protection and
of bottomless trust and of perfectness and of the paradise
of projected love; it's the end of blissful ignorance and surrender to perfection and all those dream wishes that live
in the hearts of middle-aged people. Outside the ambivalent city throbs and worries its own ambivalence, its ambiguity, its female treacherousness which is consciousness.
The city is a conch and its bugle sounds while the Cossack closes in. It sounds to heaven the evil that betrayed
us in the park and it's the inevitable end of the one-sided
paradise. The poor Cossack: an instrument in the hand of
life; its poor sacrificial victim, pray to the word which is
not proof against life!

And it's also the end, *ma Tante*, of your world. You
walk under your parasol with your adopted nephew in
your own paradise; you betray my aesthetic uncle aesthet-
ically with the conductor and sleep a paradisal sleep in the

blue of his eyes. But did you tell your nephew about the small hotel room below the gardens, the cheap wallpaper, the dirty towels, the stinking lavs, the stale liquor, the headache, the maid bringing coffee and laughing abuse at the consumption-racked woman in the hairy arms of a pot-bellied tramp with only a weather-beaten blue uniform to his name — an ape of Johann Strauss, a drinker of rank wine that you confused with Rhine wine?

There is a primitive, atavistic trust in the rock of ages crumbling away beneath the feet of the Cossack and his henchmen. Why did you not tell me? Why not? You were a sentimental mother, *ma Tante*, and even you did not realize that your betrayal had meaning. I was the noise at the window, the rustling at the door, the ear at the lowing keyhole while you vainly tried to recapture that paradise.

Or could it possibly have been what the words on your deathbed meant: "That's not what I meant, Y. Y. That's not what I meant"? Were you trying indirectly to make me aware of inevitable evil from the left?

I should like to think it was so, Aunt of mine — for the sake of my memories of you, for the sake of my longing to retain everything while the Cossack closes in and looms up enormous before my eyes and even my Russian grows uneasy and looks up into his eyes: the eyes of the Cossack. The soft eyes of the cruel god filled with compassion.

My Russian saw him as her hair fell over me; I saw him through the waterfall of her hair. His gorillas grinned like demons from hell, because they are numbers and don't bear the responsibility of his brutal decisions.

✻

I am writing like someone with a paint brush. I don't know how much is revealed in the stroke of a paint brush. (Miss X could reveal an eternity in a stroke of tender green.)

Miss X, Angélique, Princess Ira von Liebenstein, 18 years old, nineteen today according to your letters . . . I sent you perfume: a blue fragrance, because you see everything in terms of colors. What do you look like? Where is 4 Park Lane? Which park do you now range as I did twenty-six years ago? Among which swimming pools, slides and mandala merry-go-rounds do you compose your melancholy letters?

"Pray for me, Mr. Y."

"Pray harder, Mr. Y."

How deadly is the arrow that pierces the navel of the naked virgin in your drawing?

In the eyes of the Cossack, as big as the moon, like the eyes of my aunt above the rosebushes (his bullies armored monsters in white shirts), I can see the reflection of his and my Russian. We are both powerless in the clutches of mutual comprehension. Which of us is capable, at the instant preceding violence, of plucking the Russian from her sunny paradise?

"The white soldier must be shamed."

"The white soldier must be saved."

Both the Cossack and I must see that the next moment is not without meaning.

His machines stepped up close, but did not solve the problem. They plucked me from her arms, lifted me high, and smashed me to the ground.

❖

Before her eyes and the eyes of the Cossack the hack was scientifically beaten to a pulp. One could take a certain clinical satisfaction in the way they executed their task. From another point of view, one could also find some interest in the way the hack raised his arms incorrectly and got a blow in the stomach; lowered his arms and sustained a lightning flash between the eyes. (He was naturally unaware of tearing skin, of blood welling up against yet another recalcitrant skin and finally spurting out merrily as the last paper-thin fortress gave way.) A kick in the ribs breaks ribs, but it cannot be seen. A kick in the bladder has later consequences. A kick on the forehead does not shatter the brain, but it leaves a blood-red frown. A karate blow convulses the neck; a blow on the liver leaves internal injuries; a powerful shove leaves no mark, but it sends the object spinning over the lawn like a top to the feet of some magenta cannas.

The toll-claimers of our time are very much better than the toll-claimers of former times. They know exactly where to hit. It's actually a triumph of modern science: physiology for the masses.

Among the whirling spots I could see four pairs of eyes fixed on me — four pairs of eyes, windows to four souls, inexorable in their scrutiny of the act of creation in this destruction, the disintegration out of which someday, slowly, everything would have to be built up anew. I could see the sunny park of my consumption-racked aunt through the blood in my eyes: all the pagodas, all the playgrounds, all the little corners that she gave me with all the excitement of her own childlike imagination. The park was being knocked to smithereens; the park was disintegrating and being strewn over the mighty city — the trees, the flowers, the crystal earth — to become part of the dreadful city. There was no stopping it. Parks are destroyed and useless buildings pulled down in the name of progress. Cossacks and their huge henchmen swing their fists in the name of destruction and creation. With each fist blow the truth was being knocked into me and with my ravaged body I learned to love my cruel father; I understood the lack of feeling in the four pairs of eyes of four women who gazed treacherously in cold love upon the inevitable mutilation.

One is often ungrateful when a necessary injustice is happening to one; I was thankful for the form of this transcendentalism. The Cossack had picked the best gorillas; my four treacherous women had dimensions of subtlety that transcended my wildest dreams. I was truly happy. My creative acceptance of their treachery filled me with greater ambition, while I sweated blood with pain, to betray them also in my turn in the name of life.

Miss X, the fourth of the four pairs of eyes . . . I choose you first, because you are the youngest. Are you unbelievably, unattainably beautiful? But it is of no importance — even if you are as tortured and twisted as a wild fig tree. We shall sleep together in the wilderness and kill each other and heal each other under the dark, starless nights of two periods in time that have only the dark in common . . .

The first blows thudded and our nights were being knocked to ribbons thanks to the effectiveness of the powerfully alive gorillas. (Shall I make you a bet, Miss X?

Your letters will grow fewer and fewer. With finesse, fewer and fewer . . .)

I suddenly realize: I shall be forty-five tomorrow.

My sincere thanks to the strong bullies, the capable gorillas who beat to death the headstrong child a day before his birthday in the middle-aged man. Beat a child hard enough and then he will grow big; chuck him in the ditch, stamp on his head, and he'll be dead.

I have a last glimpse of Valkyrie eyes. Blue eyes like deep ice. Eighteen years of blue eyes against the background of an exuberant old man who slithered in the blood of his frozen butchery. The old man of blood who overcame ice and used it for commercial purposes alone. My poor snow goddess! He took your ice and left you with his blood. He was a little too much for us, the dealer in carcasses, because he could work both with blood and ice.

It's all over! It's all over!

The gorillas looked anxiously at their soiled white shirts; the Cossack peeped into my eyes before I forgot him and took my pulse; the Russian looked at her white soldier and did not know whether to rejoice or mourn. And then she started keening a lament: the refuge of all Slavic women when life becomes incomprehensible.

NINETEEN FORTY-FIVE was a tremendous year, an eventful year, and it was also the year the emperor was humiliated. The god becomes man: a breakthrough into another level of consciousness; an initiation on a cruiser into a world of reality after all the blood and suffering; the birth of a new tragedy; the death of primeval trust; the emancipation of evil; the indirect awakening while the woman appears beside the man and Eros destroys for good the repulsive ignorance of the past with blood, treachery and repulsiveness. The soldier of the state, in his open-necked shirt on the battleship, little realized that when he destroyed and humiliated the emperor-god, he put an end to the paradise. Millions of middle-aged people, all the 44-year-olds twenty years later, remnants of the blood conflict, will seek, uncomprehending, the paradise that is no more in 18-year-olds. The soldier of the state signed his name with a flourish. And a new life began.

I saw children's faces about me, Miss X, when I awoke in the park. It was closing time and the gates had to be locked. The irascible gardener bundled them out of the park and looked for the umpteenth time at the umpteenth wreck that he had to remove. He helped me to my feet with all the strength of his own mean body and with all the contempt tempered by service to an invisible authority. He was a little man with an enormous mustache and he was very proud of his uniform. His ten children were all thriving and drove him to madness with their buzz bikes, mini cars and guitars. He could not give a damn about what happens, because everyone has enough to eat and he no longer bears them any responsibility — only to his park which has to be cleared of wrecks every evening.

(While he sleeps peacefully at night, rape, murder, incest and immorality take place. But the following morning, thank God, everything is clean as a pin and his only problem is the cannas and the lawns.)

He led me to the gate. He led me into the street and was rid of the responsibility that municipal regulations demand of him.

Drunk people, sick people, insane people have something in common: behind the wheel of a car they become part of the city and its rhythm.

I sent my Lancia, Miss X, through all the green lights, across the crossings, with the power of the enormous machine mine to command, and I roamed through the city and its one-way streets until I reached the suburbs and found the mountain road that led to the pure sea and the little white cottage built by my friend the homosexual architect.

Princess Ira von Liebenstein among the heather . . .

Jesus . . .

All along the mountain pass, among the heather and the wild geraniums that smell like puff adders. Proteas, heather, rocks, wildflowers, weeds, empty bottles and paper . . .

Miss X, Miss X, Miss X! Did you think that betrayal is limited to the no man's land of the psyche, that indefinable world of pure spirit? That's not true. One finds its dregs in objects as well. Everything becomes stripped until one is left with lifeless science: floor, fauna and geology.

Past the place where the car plunged down the cliffs into the sea of death . . .

(The sea of death, like the road of death, takes its name from all the people who have died at sea and on the road.)

It's a wild coast where sea currents grind and waves beat on impossible places at high tide.

I found my white cottage, built by my friend the homosexual architect, empty. I called to the servants, but it was their day off. I wandered through my cottage and I suddenly realized how exposed it was; there was not a single crevice in which to hide. There were unbroken glass windows and white walls and an unexpected view over the sea, and I understood my Valkyrie's longing for the colors of her father's butchery and the security of louvers, green walls, thick doors, ox blood and heavy carcasses.

I wandered through my house, through the very clean bathroom, through the American kitchen, the neat guest room, up to a mirror in which I saw myself.

Jesus . . .

I drank a whiskey and soda and gazed at myself again. The light was good, the mirror true.

I went to my desk where my "manuscripts" lay piled up and I realized immediately . . . There was something pathetic in the way she had tried to rearrange everything. Did she think for a moment, my poor Teutonic wife, that something like that would escape the eyes of a writer: the only neatness he commands, the order of his particular chaos?

I looked over the desk at the wild sea, the stormy waves at high tide, and I limped and scrambled down the beach path as well as I could.

On the way, stumbling through the wet white sand, damp and warm with the water where the nuns had played, I looked myopically into the distance . . .

Had she read all the letters (as I dragged along limply because of the Cossack)? Did she recognize your letters, Miss X? Those extracts, those corresponding extracts? Had the daughter of a Swartland butcher-father realized enough? Can a butcher-daughter, can Valkyries accept betrayal while even my Russian, with her tremendous past of suffering, cannot?

I saw the tracks of her crutches in the sand and I saw her in front of the desk: first the curiosity and then gradual comprehension as she came upon references to the same sentences she had possibly dreamed about the previous night when she went to sleep with the letter from her cricket hero under her pillow. Was it rage that made her take up her crutches on that blind journey to the wild beach? Or was her heart broken like my aunt's about the treachery of life, or like my Russian's as her white soldier accepted humiliation without a challenge? Questions and questions and questions, Miss X, because the answer is known only to ourselves. Who am I, hack, to say whether my beloved will take refuge in denial, or cynicism, or self-destruction?

I looked myopically into the distance and I saw . . .

I saw the mist coming over the ocean: a mighty cloud that would wipe out everything in a soft white world of white invisibility, a soft mantle of oblivion under which the maelstroms and the long waves would froth among the sharks' teeth of this dangerous coast. I saw how the light in the west was being extinguished to make way for the pitch-black night so that no one could see anything and only the sounds of the night would remain. I stumbled over the sand covered with hearts drawn by lovers, with the footsteps of bronze heroes and the clover imprints of sea nymphs. Everywhere lay scattered signs of children playing their games of make-believe: a castle melting away, a fort in ruins, a broken dam wall, an oar drifting out on its way to sea, a piece of mirror with a cracked heaven.

I cursed the innocent Cossack while I stumbled through the sand and over rocks and found behind every rock nothing but the smear of foam that erases the day's tracks. I was prepared to do penance — any kind of reconciliation as long as my beloveds would be able to realize that not one among us is safe, that we all stand in the middle of life, and that even this hack, beaten into humility by the Cossack and his henchmen, will accept his inevitable guilt.

I looked myopically into the distance of the beach that was rapidly losing its outlines and I prayed that my Valkyrie would yet find something of the warm blood of her butcher-father (also misjudged in his own way). That she would feel a creative prickle in herself, if only at the level of his queens — a creative acceptance of all that is incomprehensible and ambiguous — and that at the last moment she would choose life above the paradise of her colored lights, and above the cricket heroes in the make-believe land of her childhood strand.

The weather forecast was confirmed and the thick mist rolled its own waves over the land. I hobbled and stumbled like my Valkyrie on her crutches past rocks and knee deep in icy water in my fight against the shrinking horizon. And I saw . . .

I saw her clearly, a black lithograph in the distance, the stilettos of her crutches, the pendulum of her feet. She moved over the rocks, to the coast of death where journalists from Sunday papers keep their night watch with beer, brandy and black coffee.

I was a rugby player hastening to the goal line with a torn ligament; I was a cricket player stumbling over the wicket with a lame hamstring; I was her hero, the sportsman, breaking over rocks and through sea bamboo to keep her in sight. And what a triumph it was for the hack when he was in time! In time to see her crutches like wings, horizontal over the coast of death.

My Valkyrie was always elegant; her movements were never awkward. But at that moment . . .

I saw my Valkyrie while she destroyed herself totally.

I granted her that much: the false suffering, the falsity of her colored lights that falsify truth. I granted her all falsity and unreality in her last moments. I granted her her illusion that she could attain instant success.

In that lost moment I had to be generous. And I would be generous! I granted her her lost paradise. But what happened in myself? What happens inside the Jewish father who says, "Jump!" to his son and does not catch him.

I said to her, "Jump!" — and what would the Jewish father have said if his son had killed himself? There was Abraham, Isaac and the angel. But where is my angel?

She jumped, my Valkyrie, out of this world that Douglas MacArthur revealed to us on board the battleship on the infinite ocean.

I was right next to her, and could see everything clearly.

She jumped, my poor Valkyrie, her awkward jump, because she was a cripple. She disappeared at the last moment, tail in the air, into the rhythm of the tide.

I, the reconciler, stood naked and helpless before life which is ambivalent. My heart was in shreds, but my heart was false.

I watched her crutches bobbing on the foam and then disappearing into the mist.

Father Abraham! Father Abraham!

I bet you knew, of course you knew, that God would not desert you.

AND NOW only you and I are left, Miss X, and for all practical purposes we also differ a hundred and one years from each other; in other respects we are possibly nearer to each other than ever before. All of us. Because everything was a stage of development within ourselves. Life is simply like that: our guilt, our penance is directed to God; the complete unfoldment of existing and becoming reconciled to life takes place on a cosmic plane — but it reveals itself in our relationships with one another.

Tonight I am alone in the white cottage built by my friend the homosexual architect, and I look out over the disorder of my desk toward the open sea in which my Valkyrie disappeared. The South Pole lies somewhere beyond the mist that comes in regularly over the sea at this time of year; the waves are broad and high, cracking like a whip upon the shore that changes under my eyes. A sandbank will shortly change its position; soon the beach will change unrecognizably for the coming winter. My greatest desire is that my Valkyrie will find her home in the ice of the polar world and be invisibly united there with the subcontinent. I like to think of the world of ice as something like the ocean: the Great Unconscious, the microcosm and the macrocosm, the male and the female, the fathomless pool of ice where she will be united with the Omniscient Ancestor.

I look out over my desk, Miss X, out over the disorder

that is now allowed me, over your letters that now lie openly before me, and I wish that Providence might spare me the realities of life (which I now accept) just this once: that my Valkyrie might never return; that one morning, afternoon, evening or night I might not recognize the faceless remains by a ring on a finger, a necklace around a piece of bone. The servants are exuberantly noisy in the American kitchen; the snow-white cottage is collecting dust; a part of my life is disintegrating inexorably. I look at the estate of Princess Ira von Liebenstein, who is no longer there. I think of the sunny park I shall never revisit. I think of my consumption-racked aunt, who is at long last put away in her grave. I think of my Russian, who is reconciled with her Cossack to the reality of a bourgeois existence in a modern city.

I was the great reconciler, Miss X. And I was successful. I reconciled everyone with life — except my Valkyrie. And I wonder, as I sit here writing to you, which part of myself, like my Viking, could not accept life, could not comprehend betrayal. That's the blade wound that will be left in my side: the betrayal of one single incomplete part that makes total integration impossible.

Now you and I are left, Miss X. 19–45.

It's a fantastic year in which we are going to give ourselves up utterly to the beauty of life. The nature of our despair will be tested strictly according to quality. I am ready for your letters, Miss X. Shoot the uncertainties of your teenhood over the post; let your letters burn with an urge to live; sleep with all the teen-age heroes after intervarsities; and write me of your wistfulness and your feeling of incompleteness.

We live in a cruel, glorious world which is closer to

truth than all the vanished Edens that our predecessors mourn so conservatively.

Challenge them, Miss X, for the sake of the hack, and possibly you will make him capable of becoming a decent writer.

Miss X sent me nasturtiums, kissed greetings and a challenge to love even though she was too young to realize the meaning of betrayal and life fully. She sent her perfume on the pages, her dress material in envelopes, her white kisses through the post and then her letters became fewer and fewer.

18–44. 19–45.

Only you and I are left, Miss X . . .

Miss X began to comprehend the inevitability of betrayal and she stopped writing.

Miss X, teen-ager, go forth to meet life with an inward wisdom that was unknown to me. Miss X has been fertilized, as if we had slept with each other, as if I, Mercurius, the invisible mediator, could yet arouse an orgasm of life itself.

ONLY I AM LEFT. Behind my cottage there is a mountain where scrapers and bulldozers quarry deep into the flanks so that investments from the past can bear fruit.

Princess Ira von Liebenstein's estate is purified of wild-flowers and disordered heather for the sake of elegant gardens; her picture-book castle is broken down so that chrome, steel and glass can inspire students of future technical colleges. Behind the mountain lies the city that spreads lustily in the wild rate of growing prosperity. Behind the clouds through which the Boeing cleaves its way lies my beloved's land of origin, an ice bear that wanders across the firmament. The fiery horse of a Valkyrie disappears through the clouds and the sound of the jets becomes a terrifying screech in the air.

I look in front of me, and on the beach gay girls in brightly colored dresses play beach games in their inter-sectarian walk to the ecumenical congress of their societies in the city.

I raise my binoculars through which I looked into the soul of the novices, and I try to follow the darting movements of the mission girl as she flees over rocks to the water, her thighs shamelessly exposed to the light.

I put down the binoculars, pour a whiskey and soda, pick up my pen and start repairing the mutilated gift of God.

The sun shines brightly, I rechristen my zodiacal cottage Breidablick, and I start writing about resurrection and love, about primeval betrayal and a new life, about the past, the present and the future, in my striving for maturity, for a higher level of consciousness and a better comprehension of the tragedy of life.

I put down my pen and I look at the new brides of God playing in the sand.

Yes, I decided. Yes, I will.

And I pick up my pen and write a book for the four Marias around my cross on the sand.